Sleighed

M.K Vindictiv

Contents

For those wondering what it would be like
to get railed in Santa's sleigh.

Chapter One
Kris

I AM SO FUCKING sick of listening to Christmas carols.

You'd think after living in Santa's village for the last sixteen years I would be used to the year round Christmas cheer, but the older I get, the more the wonder and novelty has worn off and the more I feel myself turning into the Grinch.

When I arrived in Santa's village as a thirteen-year-old, it had felt like a totally overwhelming whirlwind. After spending so many years with just my mom, suddenly being thrown into a new family—and not just any family, but what felt like the most perfect family in existence—made me more than a little bah humbug toward the Christmas spirit.

My mom met Klaus, better known as Santa Claus to everyone else, on December twenty-fourth, sixteen years ago.

Sneaking downstairs to catch a peak at Santa led to more of an eyeful than I expected. I found my mom pinned up against the wall, Santa's tongue down her throat, underneath the mistletoe we had hung the night before.

Mom and Klaus quickly developed an obsession with each other, and by December twenty-sixth, our bags were packed, and we were on our way to relocate as far north as someone could get.

My natural response to act like a jerk was no match for the allure of being the outsider in such a tight-knit community. It didn't take long for the elves my age to flock to me, especially the girls. Even when I wanted to be left alone, it only made them work harder for my attention.

You'd think that now I am an adult the novelty of being Santa's stepson would have worn off, but it hadn't and for that my dick was incredibly thankful.

The garage door opens, letting in flurries of snow, sending chills fluttering down my spine. The sleigh above me doing little to shield me from the blustery winds that wrap around the sleigh's expansive frame with me lying beneath it.

My jaw tenses as the sound of the carols get louder, almost drowning out the music I'm blasting through the garage's stereo.

My molars grind together as I try to focus on the heavy drumbeat and the wrench in my hand, blocking out the town's festive cheer and the gray-haired elf currently examining my work.

Theodore Honey-Pickle was slowly becoming the bane of my fucking existence. Him and those damn curled shoes he insisted on tapping near my face as he waited for me to acknowledge his presence.

Ever since his promotion to Head Elf, he had taken it upon himself to do regular check-ups on the status of my progress, and my tolerance for the middle-aged tyrant was diminishing rapidly.

He picks a piece of lint off his bright green elf uniform. The gold trim marking him as Head Elf glittered as he slowly walks around the sleigh jotting notes on his parchment.

If I grit my teeth any harder, I was likely to break one.

My forearms strain, gripping the wrench tighter in my hand. Veins pop out across the backs of my hands, traveling up the corded muscles of my forearms as they flex with the strength needed to loosen the bolt holding the compressor in place.

"Are you sure you will have the sleigh ready by the twenty-fourth, Kristopher?" His inclination to use my full name has me tensing my fingers around the wrench, my knuckles turning white as I imagine the wrench flying at his stupid face. The thought has one side of my lips curling up.

Ever since the man I was named after left on the eve of my fifth birthday, no one had called me that name, not even my mother. However, Theodore took great delight in the way I reacted every time he mentioned it.

"Yes." The wrench slips from my grasp, causing me to hiss in annoyance at both it and the elf analyzing my every move. It bangs against my fingers and crashes to the floor with a resounding clank, missing my face by mere inches. "Fuck!"

Using the rails for support, my back flush with the creeper as I slide myself out from underneath the bottom of the sleigh. Sitting up on the board, I rub my hands as the elf glares at me through tiny gold-rimmed spectacles. He noticeably flinches at my use of the F word.

"It's just that there's..." Theodore pushes his jacket aside, his hand reaching for the chain attached to a golden pocket watch, the lid decorated with a beautifully engraved gift box. As he yanks on the chain, it jingles softly, adding to his sense of urgency. "Only 109 hours left till launch and the reindeer haven't had their test flight yet," he mutters. "They were supposed to be air-bound twenty-four hours ago."

He slips the watch back into his pocket before hastily rolling out the parchment now tucked in the crook of his elbow. His to-do list would give the naughty and nice lists Klaus checks every year a run for their money.

Paper rustles as he rifles through the scroll, muttering to himself. I ignore his ramblings, finding amusement in the way the tips of his ears turn pinker the more frazzled he gets.

I stand, placing one foot up against the sleigh railing as I lean back, pulling a packet of cigarettes out from the back pocket of my overalls. The packet is slightly squished after the hours I've spent under the hood.

Not bothering to wipe my fingers free of the grease, I pull out a smoke and hold it between my lips. My lighter flicks open with a satisfying click and seconds later the tip of the cigarette glows brightly as I inhale, feeling slightly calmer as the smoke moves through my lungs.

"Stop stressing, *Theodore*. I told you it would be done." The smoke escapes from my lips, slithering into the air, backlit by the glow of the fairy lights as I answer.

"I just want everything to go smoothly for your brother's first run. Christmas Eve is already so important, but his first as Santa Claus," he says the name with such reverence, I could vomit. "Everything needs to be perfect." His voice breaking on the last words, nearly jumping up an octave, as his agitation gets the better of him.

Theodore has always been Klaus' most trusted elf, his promotion was more of a formality than anything else. Even when I first moved to the village he could always be found rushing around doing all the jobs of Head Elf. He knows the ins and outs of the Christmas business like the back of a gingerbread house.

"I will make sure it is done in time," I say, my voice becoming harsh, enunciating each word as I push myself up from the sleigh.

"And if my *step*brother has any complaints, he knows where to find me." I say, heavily emphasizing the step, before gesturing to the sixty-foot red and gold sleigh parked behind me.

Theodore huffs, practically stomping his feet with the exhalation. I use the back of my hand to wipe at my mouth, attempting and failing to disguise my smirk at the tiny jingle that comes from his shoes.

Already feeling done with this conversation, I ignore the elf's further complaints and walk over to my workbench and crank the stereo. The heavy thrashing of guitars drown him and the remaining sounds of carols out.

Leaning back against the workbench, I stare at a red faced Theodore, as he tries to shout over the now deafening music. I mime my inability to hear him mouthing "I can't hear you" before pushing back the sweat dampened hair that is hanging limply in my eyes, taking another drag of my cigarette.

Theodore scrambles to roll up his parchment, his mouth pressed into a firm line as his eyes shoot daggers through me. He shakes his head, turning with a flourish and stomping out of the garage as he slams the door behind him.

I'm sure he is on his way to tell Klaus I am being uncooperative, but it's not like his opinion of me has ever been positive. Why start now?

Last Christmas, when Klaus announced his retirement, it didn't come as a surprise to anyone. After all, he had been doing the job for over five decades. He stood next to the sleigh, snow still dusting his thick white beard, staring lovingly at my mother. They were both ready for some downtime. To spend their lives supporting Christmas, rather than being the star of the show.

His announcement rang out cheers from the crowd, confirming once and for all that he was passing the reins to my stepbrother Nick, also not a surprise.

From the time I set foot in the village, everyone hailed Nick as the future of Christmas, the pride of our family.

With my heavy metal tunes blaring and my carefree attitude, I stood out as the outsider, dampening the Christmas cheer. The village's very own Scrooge.

The people in the village meticulously planned and cultivated everything. Children followed their parents into family run careers and everything kept rotating like a never ending wheel of doom.

I was a wrench in the cog of their uniformity. I didn't fit. Since Nick would follow in our parents' footsteps, what job could they possibly assign to me?

That is how I landed in the garage. Well, almost.

At seventeen, I had taken it upon myself to offer the village some *redecorating* in the form of a new mural painted on the side of the sleigh garage.

I was standing back, admiring my handiwork, taking in the scene of a female elf being spit roasted by two reindeer. The garage door suddenly swung open and Arthur, the current sleigh mechanic, emerged.

I froze, waiting for the backlash, but Arthur just assessed my painting skills and chuckled to himself before clasping me on the back, inviting me into his workshop.

The tools were mesmerizing, and I had found a purpose in being able to make something useful again with my hands.

When the sleigh wasn't in need of maintenance, we ensured all the village machines and transportation were up and running.

My first job, after repainting the garage wall before anyone could see it, was to touch up the paint on the sleigh decals. The gold swirls were intricate and detailed, and I found myself entranced.

From then on I had spent every moment I wasn't required at school or with my family locked in this shed, fixing, building, painting.

I couldn't stop my mind from slipping back to Nick. Despite his inevitable path following his father, I had no genuine issues with him.

The only thing that bothered me was the way my chest tightened and ached whenever he was close to me, and the fact my dick never forgot to remind me of his existence.

An insatiable, constant, gnawing sensation that never went away.

I had fucked my way through half of the elves my age, men and women alike, but there was something about the stupid fucking twinkle in Nick's eye whenever he caught me looking at him, that had my fists clenching with the sudden need to throw him over my knee and spank the shit out of his ass till it was as red as the tip of Rudolph's nose.

My thoughts snapped back to reality as the door swung back open with a crash and Arthur entered, lugging in a bunch of unknown sleigh parts.

"I just saw Teddy tearing through the middle of the village," he said with a chuckle, "that wouldn't have anything to do with a visit to you now would it?"

I shrug, and huffing out a laugh, took one last drag on my smoke and put it out in the empty beer can on my bench. "*Teddy* seems to have his panties in a twist that we won't finish in time."

Grabbing one of the new air filters from Arthur's cart, I lay myself back on the creeper and push myself back under the sleigh. The four-foot elf stops my gliding and drags me back out, now peering down at me in grease stained overalls.

"You called him Theodore, didn't you?" The shit-eating grin that split my face makes his shoulders bounce with his contained laughter and he shakes his head.

"You're an asshole, you know that."

"Hey! I'll stop calling him Theodore when he stops calling me Kristopher." Arthur's smile softens as he looks me over and I move to push myself back under the sleigh, to avoid this touchy feely moment but I'm once again pulled back out.

"Sorry son, but you've been summoned to join everyone up at the house." His pitying look has me turning away. He, more than anyone, knew how uncomfortable I felt in that house.

Though I was still required to live there, Arthur was always the first to provide me with cover to get out of as many things as I could as a teen, but now at twenty-nine there was no escaping.

Fucking great. Nothing like dinner with the family.

This is going to be a long fucking Christmas.

Chapter Two
Nick

"CAN YOU TAKE THOSE potatoes to the table, love?" Carol, my stepmother, hands me an enormous bowl of butter drenched mashed potatoes.

"Sure." With a gentle kiss on the cheek, she hands me the hot bowl, and I can feel the heat radiating through my fingers.

She cups my cheek and thanks me, her eyes lingering on the stubble that's appearing. "You're becoming more and more like your father." Making a humming noise, she runs her hand over the rough salt and pepper hairs that are sadly looking more salt than pepper. A family trait or so I've been told.

Whenever I hear the comparison, my heart constricts with a mix of emotions. In the lineage of Santa Claus, my father holds the record for being the youngest Santa Claus ever, while I, at thirty-one, am poised to become the oldest Santa Claus in history.

When his father suddenly died on his way back to the North Pole on Christmas Day, my father was forced to take over the role at barely eighteen.

Although this time of year is what we spent the entire year working towards, it is tainted with an incredible amount of sadness for my father. The loss he experienced only grew worse when we tragically lost my mother in a sledding accident during the week leading up to Christmas, when I was just ten-years-old.

Losing two of the most important people in his life had made him feel bitter about the whole thing. I even remembered a time when he debated quitting and letting another family take over the role.

That was the year he met Carol. Their whirlwind romance had blown us all away, and after more than a decade, they were still so utterly in love. I guess when you meet the right person, you just know.

I often found myself jealous of their love, having a person to come home to and share your life with. I had assumed I would just find somebody. By my age, my father had already settled down with my mother, who lived in a nearby village, and I was on my way into the world.

I had zero prospects.

My future title, as Santa Claus, intimidated everyone too much to even attempt anything romantic with me. Sure, everyone wanted to fuck the future Santa, but in reality, no one wanted to stick around and love him.

I made my way through the kitchen to the dining room table. My thoughts spinning about my future came to a crashing halt when the front door flew open and my stepbrother Kris walks in.

As he enters the dining room, my jaw drops open involuntarily. I'm captivated by the sight of him, bare chested with his overalls tied loosely around his waist. My eyes lock on his tight pecs, which almost seem to flex under my scrutiny.

My eyes betray me as they continue their inspection, lowering to the smooth muscles of his abs that cut sharply in. A path for my eyes to follow, leading directly to the spot I was aching for but forbidden to touch.

I wasn't sure if my brain had imagined the light dusting of dark hair at the end of that v, or if his overalls were tied so low that it could be seen.

The smear of grease that traveled from his collarbone over to one nipple made me lick my lips. I could imagine his calloused hands marking my body, making me as dirty as he is.

Tripping, I stumble into the dining chair before not so casually catching myself and placing the potatoes into the middle of the table. Thanking every God that I didn't throw a bowl of steaming mash all over myself.

Looking up, I gave Kris a quick nod, trying my best to ignore the smirk tugging at the corner of his lips, and the way his gaze traveled down my body before stopping on the bulge now growing in my suit pants.

"Kris," Carol exclaimed as she came through the large entryway into the dining room, causing me to jump. Carrying a roast chicken on a large platter, which she hands to me so she can properly greet her son. I take the distraction to gather my incredibly stupid thoughts as I place it on the table next to the mash.

"Hey Ma." The husky timbre of his voice has me gripping the back of the chair to stop myself from drifting towards him. I don't know what it was about Kris, but he had always pulled these reactions from my body.

When Kris first moved in I had thought it was just a hormone response, my need to explore my body like any normal teenager, that had me jerking into my fist multiple times a day.

In school, we were told it was normal to develop sexual attractions towards people, but we were never told how to react when that person was not only of the same sex but living under the same roof.

How could my feelings ever be normal if they were towards someone who not only was the most breathtaking man I'd ever seen, but also someone who now most people in the village referred to as my brother?

I told myself when I met the right girl, these feelings would disappear. Sixteen years on and I still jerked into my fist regularly over the thought of what he could do to me.

Swallowing the lump caught in my throat, I excused myself to the kitchen to grab some water. Kris' jade green eyes locking on mine as I crossed the room.

A few minutes later, I stood at the stove stirring the gravy as Carol entered back in.

"Oh Nick, you didn't have to finish that." I shrug.

"It's fine Carol, my pleasure." Looking around the room and noting Kris' absence, "Where is Kris?"

"Oh, he just ran upstairs to clean up before dinner. Don't want to get grease all over Grandma Holly's favorite table cloth." Humming we wish you a merry Christmas, as she applied the finishing touches to the last of the vegetables. We work in companionable silence as we both mull around the kitchen.

Though I'm sure her thoughts aren't filled with the dripping wet man washing himself in the bathroom above us.

"Are you ready for the big night, my boy?" My father asked, shoving another fork full of roasted meat into his mouth. His voice naturally booming so loud it just about shook the crystalware off the table.

"Of course, Father. You've been preparing me my whole life for this. I'm more than ready."

I didn't feel ready.

In fact, I felt so far from ready I would be more than happy to pack a bag and go live off the land never to be seen from again, but as a Claus I had no other option.

"What are your plans for tomorrow?" My father's cheeks appeared redder tonight. They usually had a rosy hue to them but the butterscotch brandy he had been drinking all meal had clearly taken its effect, adding more color to his cheeks and a slur to his words.

I have never seen my father drunk before. As Santa Claus, his life ran on schedules and routine. The need to be available at any moment for an emergency had taken its toll on his spontaneity, and the carefree man now sitting at the end of the table almost felt like a stranger.

"I have a meeting with Teddy in the morning to discuss where we are in the preparations, a walk through the workshop to oversee any final making and wrapping of presents, and probably finishing my night off with one last check through the list." I rattled off, using my napkin to wipe away any gravy from my lips, catching Kris staring at the movement out of the corner of my eye.

The list was sure to turn my already graying hair white by Christmas Eve.

How could one decide if a child had been good or not? What was the line of no return for a child to be moved to the naughty list? Is a child who forgets their chores destined for the same fate as one who intentionally sets their neighbor's yard on fire?

The stress of making the right call was sure to give me an aneurysm by the time Christmas Eve came.

"Good, good," my father praised. "A Claus' work is never done. Enjoy it my boy, this will be a week you will never forget. Your first Christmas will always be your most special."

A small scoff came from the other side of the table and all our eyes landed on Kris, leaning back, one arm slung casually over the chair and pushing peas back and forth around his plate. His still damp hair hanging over his face in messy onyx curls just like his mother's.

Although unlike his mother's long curly locks, Kris kept his hair cropped shorter at the sides, keeping the top longer so the curls nestled across his forehead in haphazard waves that made him look like he had either just climbed out of bed or spent hours styling them to lie in just the right spot.

"Something to add, Kris?" My father's eyes turn hard, eyebrows raising. The soft, playful nature that had surrounded him as Santa Claus seemed lost on Kris.

They had a knack for butting heads, and it seemed like they couldn't agree on anything, no matter the topic.

"No, sir." He waves his finger in mock salute, not even bothering to look up from his food.

My father straightens in his chair, his whole body stiffening as he took in Kris.

His band tee with the sleeves cut off covered most of the muscles I had stared at for far too long before, only a sliver of skin showing on each side of his ribs and his chiseled arms.

Just by looking at Kris you could tell he spent all day working with his hands. His forearms had a definition to them that I could only dream of. Sculpted with deep veins noticeable as he grips his fork tighter, fully aware of the scrutiny that he's now under.

"Since you're so eager to join the conversation, Kris, how is the sleigh going?" My father's grip turns white against the wide bottom of his brandy glass, waiting for Kris' response.

"It's going."

"That is not what I have been hearing." My father huffs into his glass as he takes a deep pull of the amber liquid.

"Oh." Kris drops his fork and stares up at my father, a challenge radiating in his eyes, "And what have you been hearing, Klaus?"

"That you have been fucking half of the elf population and too busy to actually get the one job we trusted you to complete on time?" Spit flies from my father's mouth, his jarring words startling Carol enough to drop her own fork as she covers her mouth.

"Jeez. I'm surprised old Theodore could even get those words out, since he practically cried when I said the word fuck this afternoon." His casual words fell in stark contrast to his body language, poised ready to fight my father.

"I can't believe I even trusted you with such an important job. You'd think at twenty-nine you would have gotten your shit together enough to actually show some responsibility around here." Kris' fists clench on the table before he pulls them out of sight, dropping them to his lap.

"I had higher hopes for you, but I guess the apple doesn't fall far from the useless tree." Carol gasps at the jab of Kris' biological father.

The way Kris' dad left Carol and him to fend for themselves was not something we ever discussed. It was a low blow, even for him.

Carol's eyes flick over to Kris, tears brimming her lashes as she inhales a small shuddering breath before attempting to excuse herself from the table.

My father, realizing his mistake, places a hand over his wife's before she could stand. Rubbing his thumb in circles as he speaks to her, hushed whispers of apology, soothing the burn of his careless words.

My attention drifts back to Kris, who sits silent, glaring a hole through the table, his knife and fork gripped tightly in his hands.

Although it wasn't the right time for indulging in fantasies, I couldn't help but imagine his large, rough hands firmly holding onto my pulsing dick, his forearms displaying the sculpted muscles he had developed through the daily use of his tools.

His gaze slowly drifts up, looking between my father and Carol and dropping to their joined hands, lip curling as Carol nods something in agreement with my father.

Slamming back his chair, the legs scrape across the hardwood floors in an ear splitting squeak, the glassware shuddering under his movement.

"Fuck this." He spits, pulling a cigarette out of his pocket and lighting it. Drawing in a lung full before blowing it dramatically over the table.

"Kris?" my father stammers, his eyes pleading.

Kris, threw one hurt look back at his mom before flipping off the table over his head as he made his exit.

"Merry FUCKING Christmas," he barks back before slamming the front door so hard the windowpanes rattle.

Chapter Three

Nick

After Kris' dramatic exit, Carol continued to cry silently next to me. I place a soothing hand on her back before standing and gathering everyone's dishes as my father coos his apologies in her ear.

Normally, the sight would make me feel jealous, wishing for a love like theirs. Now I felt a burning anger and the need to protect Kris.

I understood the pressure to ensure that everything ran smoothly this week, but calling Kris out implying he was useless, like his deadbeat father, was a low blow.

I clean the dishes in silence, staring out the window at the snow covered paradise that was my village. My father and Carol continue to speak in hushed voices in the other room. My anger simmers with every passing minute.

After what felt like nearly an hour had passed, Carol joins me in the kitchen, eyes now red and blotchy.

"Thank you Nick. I appreciate your help tonight." She gives me a weak smile as she takes the snowflake covered tea towel from my hands and picks up the last platter from the sink.

"I just don't know what to do for him. Haven't we given him everything?" Her voice breaking as she pauses, leaning onto the counter, closing her eyes as her shoulders drop.

"I have been hearing great things about him too, Carol." She looks back at me with a glimpse of fractured hope. "All reports that have come to me say he is one of the best mechanics we have. If he says the sleigh will be ready on time, I trust him." That was the truth. I would trust Kris with my entire world if only I had the guts to give it to him.

She quickly gathered me up in the same warm embrace she had given me since I was fifteen. Still grieving for a mother while trying to welcome a new family.

"I am so proud of you, Nick. You have turned into a fine man and will be an excellent Santa Claus."

"Maybe Kris just needs a bit more of your trust, too. Yes, he differs from most here in the village, but he has his own ways. They aren't necessarily wrong, they just aren't the way everyone is used to doing them around here."

Carol nods her understanding as she turns back to the sink, wiping it free of the soapsuds that have gathered.

My heart drops at the thought of Kris, alone and upset, out in the garage working on my sleigh. The sudden pang of need to go and check on him overtaking me.

I grab my jacket and scarf from the back of the kitchen door, wrapping them around me. The sight of his jacket hanging on the hook next to mine had me remembering that Kris had walked out of the house in nothing but a muscle tee earlier.

Despite my father's Christmas magic heating all the buildings in the village, the outside weather, especially at this time of year, remained bitterly cold.

The overwhelming smell of peppermint and cigarettes hits me as I pull his jacket from the hook. The smell, so intoxicating, I can't help but bury my nose into the black wool, inhaling deeply. Closing my eyes, I will my dick to not react to his familiar scent. The smell solidifying my resolve to make sure he was okay.

"I'll be back in a while." Carol turns at the sink, looking at me, brows furrowing.

"Where are you going?" she questioned, "There is a storm coming later."

Part of me debates telling her I forgot something at the office, but the other part of me assures my brain that even though I had constant dreams about sucking her son's dick, there was nothing wrong with my checking on my brother.

"I'm gonna go check on Kris." I nod and pull the back door open. Opting to walk through the backyard, not wanting to risk bumping into my father on the other side of the house. Carol's voice had me pausing before I could close the door.

"You're a good brother, Nick."

Kris' scent wrapped around my cock as I stood in the doorway looking back at the same shade of green that has haunted my dreams since I was fifteen.

I didn't feel like a very good brother.

I find myself taking the long way to the garage. Our little winter village is beautiful, especially at night, when the snow settles after the bustling activity of the day.

The town square with a red and white lamppost in the center marks the Northern most spot of the world. Fairy lights cover every inch of roofing and railing and spreads to the center, meeting in a spiral at the very tip of the post.

As the year gets closer to Christmas, our decorations become more extravagant.

The Christmas tree, a one hundred foot pine, dragged down by the reindeer from the top of the mountains that surround us, marks the start of our holiday season. The tree was a magnificent sight to behold as it stands tall at the heart of the village. Its branches are adorned with countless lights that form a mesmerizing wave of brightness, ending with a dazzling golden star at the very top.

Tinsel and baubles decorate every window, and the constant wafting of hot chocolate and gingerbread fills the air. Even at the end of the holiday season, the lights remain on the buildings all year round, still making this place feel magical long after the snow melts.

I had never realized just how magical this place was in my teens. I was itching to see the world, experience somewhere else.

That was until Kris arrived with his mom. The wonder that crossed his face made me develop a newfound appreciation for the village I had spent my entire life in.

Funny how, now the thought of leaving my home in four days, even if only for one night, made me want to hurl.

With snow crunching underfoot, my focus lands on the garage. It was wrapped in the same Christmas lights as every other building but still a yellow glow poured through the window, like a beacon calling me.

The distant sound of Kris' metal music reached my ears on the breeze, a clear indication that he was still locked inside, engrossed in his work.

My hands wrap around the handle to pull the door open, but I freeze when a guttural moan cries out through the cold steel. My brain is second guessing what it just heard, but my cock certainly doesn't as it springs to life, pressing hard against my zipper, causing a small whimper to slip from my mouth.

The side window sits to my right and I move towards it on instinct, using the sleeve of my jacket to wipe away the snow dusting over the windowpane.

My throat bobs, mouth watering at the sight in front of me.

Kris stands half naked, bare ass pressed into the side of the sleigh, head tipped back in pleasure.

I know I should turn away but I can't. This sight isn't meant for me, though I can't deny the heat rising in my body as my hand palms my growing erection.

Biting my lip, I watch him swallow as another groan leaves his lips. He uses one hand to push back the stray curl that has fallen across his face. My eyes track every movement of his muscles down the length of his torso, tensing and flexing as he pushes forward.

That's when I realize I've been too absorbed in my own thoughts to notice that Kris is not alone.

On her knees in front of him is Pepper, one of the line elves from the workshop.

Now I know I should leave. Watching Kris is bad enough but watching him roughly pound into the mouth of one of my employees is definitely not in any of the employer handbooks my father has made me pour over.

Kris leans against the side of the sleigh, his tee still on but his ripped jeans pool at his ankles, one hand presses against the side of the sleigh and the other firmly gripping into Pepper's hair.

She sits naked in front of him, her arms bound tightly behind her back with tinsel, straddling the life size outdoor snowman that usually stands proudly at the entrance to the garage.

The snowman glows, still lit up from within as Pepper grinds herself back and forth over its smiling face, the inflatable carrot nose rubbing against her clit with each slow grind.

I take a second to get over the shock of seeing one of my employees pleasuring herself on one of the town square decorations, but my attention naturally finds its way back to Kris.

His abs flex every time the base of his cock hits the back of her throat. The sight has me panting, pushing myself up against the wall, desperate for any friction.

He doesn't even look at her while she goes to town on him, even though her body is on full display for him, clearly eager for him to fuck her.

Instead, he casually leans against my sleigh, running his hand across the gleaming red paint as the four-foot elf sucks his cock with vigor.

Though it would be absurd to think that as he closes his eyes, that it's my mouth he is thinking about, the feeling of my lips wrapped around him. Even though I know it's not possible, my imagination misses the memo and runs wild with fantasies.

Her moans increase as she nears her peak. By the way he clenches her hair harder, the vibrations of her cries must be helping to build him closer to the edge, too.

As the wind picks up and my cock stiffens to the point of aching, a sudden wave of jealousy builds in my chest.

Before I know what I am doing, I storm towards the garage doors, my cock is about to burst my seams as I throw the door open.

It takes a second for the wind and snow to reach them, alerting them to the fact that they are no longer alone.

Pepper squeals attempting to climb off of the snowman unassisted, as Kris' eyes lock on me, my chest heaving.

"Shit, Nick! Fuck." Pepper's shrill voice is clear even over the pounding music. In her haste to jump off the snowman she trips, face planting on the floor at Kris' feet, causing him to break our stare first.

He bends helping her up then adeptly unties the knot on her hands, one handed, before those jade green eyes slam back into mine again.

Both of us ignore the muttering Pepper, who is clutching her yellow tinkerer uniform as she tries to slip into her shoes. They jingle as she pauses, half slipping into her dress.

"Ah, Nick, boss. I'm ah … fuck," She stammered, running past me.

With the door slamming shut behind her, the room suddenly feels too hot.

My cock is still straining in my trousers begging for my attention, or Kris'. That thought has my eyes dropping to where his cock stands, pulsing and on display for me.

Kris doesn't even bat an eyelid at my perusal or make any attempt to cover himself. If anything, his eyes grow more heated. The jerk of his cock, suggesting he's more than happy for my eyes to drink him in.

"Well, since you just spoiled my fun for the evening, you can either pick up where she left off or get the fuck out so I can finish myself off." His tone is huskier than normal, lust coating his words.

With a tilt of his head, he leans back against the sleigh, taking his cock in one hand, showing me his intentions to follow through with his threat if I turn and walk out the door.

But for the first time in my life, I don't want to walk away and pretend this attraction doesn't exist.

For once, I'm exactly where I want to be.

His hand tightens around his length. Taking his time to run it up and down his impressive shaft. That one long stroke of his hand has me licking my lips, my cock leaking at the thought of my mouth wrapping around him. How soft his skin would feel, the taste of his cum on my tongue.

I have never touched another man's cock before, but I'm damn sure I wanted Kris to be the first. The only.

I drift towards him, his eyes widening a fraction is the only tell that he is just as affected as I am as I move closer. This showdown between us tightly gripping us both.

As I step into his space, his fingers release his length and he grabs back onto the side of the sleigh in anticipation. My stomach flutters at the thought of affecting him, half as much as he impacted me.

It was now or never. This was the opportunity I had been waiting for and if I didn't take it now, it would probably never come again.

I don't take my eyes from his as I lower to my knees, ignoring the way the cold concrete floor bites into my knees. I don't want to miss any reaction he gifts me.

His salty aroma greeted me as his cock met my face. Leaning closer, I try to hide the tremble in my fingers and wrap one hand firmly around the base of his thickness, just like I would do for myself.

A hiss of a breath through his lips is enough encouragement to spur me on, praying I'm doing this correctly. I watch him as I open my mouth wide and push my lips over his tip, not stopping till it hits the back of my throat, causing me to gag.

"Oh Fuck," Kris groaned out, breaking our stare off as his head falls back, slamming hard against the sleigh as he groans deeply. I drink in his reactions, greedy for anything he was willing to give me.

As I pullback, his hand finds its way into my hair, caressing me before gripping tightly, and I moan around his cock, dying for more of his touch.

"Ah Nick, fuck. I didn't know you were into this." He breathes out a sigh as my lips slide back off. I run my tongue along the slit before our gazes lock again, his onyx waves falling over his eyes as they bore into mine.

"I've never done this before." I admit. His eyes widen at my admission, but the way I almost ground into the floor gives away my desperate need for him. He releases his grip slightly on my hair, allowing my lips to glide back over the uncut head using my mouth to push back the skin, I eagerly suck him in.

"God, no one would ever be able to fucking guess." He moans, gently using his hand to guide me further down his length than I thought I could go. "Just breathe, you can take it."

His words calm me and I release a breath through my nose as he pushes past my gag reflex. A second later the fullness causes me to choke, and he pulls out, stroking my face.

"Good boy." He coos, shuffling one of his legs forward until it's pressed in between mine and I whimper at the feel of his foot grazing against my cock.

"Grind on my foot." His voice was demanding, his molten gaze darkening as he waited for my decision.

I didn't hesitate. I finally had him and I would take every ounce of pleasure he was willing to give me, even if it was only for tonight.

Without dropping my gaze, I move to unzip my pants.

"Uh-uh," he tsked. "Pants stay on."

Swallowing, I lifted myself over the laces of his boot, hovering for a second, then grinding myself down. My eyes flutter shut with the first movement of my hips. The pleasure my cock had been aching for finally within reach.

A whimper leaves me as he raises his foot slightly to add extra pressure to my taint. My mouth wraps around his length, in a desperate need to give him the pleasure I was feeling.

My grip on the base of his shaft tightened as I simultaneously moved my hand to keep in time with my mouth, grinding myself against his foot.

"Ah fuck, yes. Just like that." His praise has me melting, panting and grinding feverishly, desperate for more.

"Look how well you take my cock." I suck hard. His soft words and firm grip on my hair has me squirming against his boot, I'm so close to release I can feel the base of my spine tingling as it builds.

"I'm close," I pant around his cock. "So fucking close."

"Not without me." He growls as he pulls his leg away, and I whimper at the loss of friction.

Digging his fingers tighter into my hair, he takes control of my head, using me, owning me. Fucking my face at a pace I struggle to keep up with.

"I'm going to come," he says as he looks down at me, eyes burning with lust, "and you're going to swallow every last drop, like a good fucking boy and then I might let you come too, okay?"

I can't do anything but nod frantically around his cock. The cusp of my pleasure is so close, I could feel it. One more stroke and I would explode in my jeans like a boy with his first orgasm.

"Fuck!" He roars with such force it was surprising the windowpanes didn't rattle.

Warm streams of cum hit the back of my throat and my first instinct is to spit it out, but with those jade eyes watching me I could only force myself to swallow. His dick still pulsing, leaking salty cum into my mouth.

After the first swallow, it isn't too bad, and I focus on enjoying a moment we many never repeat. The fear spurs me on as I desperately lick up and down his length, using my fist to squeeze as much as I can get from his tip.

Looking down at me, his eyes darken as he smirks, admiring my handy work before shuffling his boot back between my legs, leaving his cock flexing in my face.

"Good fucking boy." Shivering at his words, I whimper at the friction his foot provides. My cock weeping, pulsing against his boot, desperate for release, but he watches me intently. "Now, come on my foot."

I release a breath I didn't realize I was holding. His permission to come has me scrambling to push against his leg, grinding against the laces of his greasy work boots.

My release quickly builds deep within me and the base of my spine begins to tingle, my whole body on fire under his instruction.

Fuck, had this been what Pepper was feeling before I interrupted them? I would have to send her a gift basket for ruining the best orgasm of her life.

With a single sweep of his hand across my hair, my spiraling thoughts cease, and I tip into oblivion. My eyes squeeze shut as I convulse against his boot. My forehead drops to his thigh, my hot sticky release fills my trousers, and I groan out his name.

His fingers pull harshly on the strands of my hair, yanking my head back so he can watch me crumble. His eyes narrow and his head tilts, that rogue curl falls across his sweat covered brow as he drinks me in. Watching me grind and whimper against his leg, trying to drag out the last of my release.

When the waves of pleasure finally calm, I sit panting on my knees. My hands fall to the floor, and a wave of guilt crashes into me. What the hell have we just done?

We haven't just crossed a line as stepbrothers; we jumped right the fuck over it.

Neither of us say anything as I get to my feet. I leave his jacket on the floor next to him. I avoid the knowing glare of the glowing snowman, who now looks at me with his fake smile and Christmas cheer, accusingly.

I don't even have the nerve to look back at him to try to gauge his reaction to this, because if I look back and see regret or God forbid pity, I would have to drag myself up the mountain and find the nearest cliff to throw myself off of.

So instead of facing the consequences of my actions, I choose to be a coward, and walk away from him.

Not even the blizzard coming from the mountains could cool the shame that burns hot through my chest as I start the long sticky walk home.

Chapter Four

Kris

I still sit in the same spot Nick left me last night after dropping to his knees and giving me the head job of my dreams before walking out and leaving me in his dust.

I had spent the night questioning every look and conversation we had ever had, wondering where I had missed the fact that Nick was into guys. Well, maybe not guys, but more specifically, me.

Though I had never been naïve to his wandering eyes, I never thought there had been genuine interest behind them, or could have anticipated the way he melted in my hands as I praised him.

Fuck, the memory of him whimpering as I took my foot away had my cock begging for round two. The feeling of exploding in his mouth and him eagerly licking it all down, even when he struggled to take it, had short-circuited something in me and now all of my thoughts centered on him.

I hadn't even bothered cleaning up last night after he walked out without so much as a glance back in my direction. I just slumped to the floor, my legs finally giving out after the adrenaline had worn off, and stayed here.

Eventually I crashed out, my head leaning against the cool metal of the sleigh, dreaming of crystal blue eyes and soft little whimpers.

Dragging my knees up and rubbing my hands over my eyes, I push my hair off my face, sighing as I looked up at the ceiling. What the fuck had we done?

The familiar weight of my cigarettes in my top pocket grounded me. The familiar routine calming me, bang, flick, breathe, relax.

I sat with my forearms resting on my bent knees and took in my workshop, smoke invading my lungs, numbing my nerves, and contemplated my next move.

Did I want to do that again with Nick? Fuck yes.

Was I sure that Nick wanted the same? No, but I would not go down without a fight.

If he thought he could walk out of here like nothing happened and I wouldn't make him see the error of his ways, he had another thing coming.

Stepbrother or not, I didn't give a fuck.

If I had it my way, Nick would be riding my dick and screaming my name by Christmas Eve.

Now I had him. There was no way I was letting him go.

The garage door swinging open suddenly interrupts my thoughts. Arthur strolls in with two coffees in his hands, the scent of peppermint wafting toward me.

"Rough night?" he questions, giving me a once over before his eyes find the snowman I had dragged in for Pepper to grind on. The tinsel I bound her hands with lays limply on the floor.

Pepper was okay, though she was far too cheery for anything more than a quick fuck. I preferred her gagged to shut her the hell up for more than five minutes. The tinsel helped with her obsession of running her hands down my body. I know she thought she was seducing me, but it was really just kinda fucking weird.

Looking over at the mess she had left in her abrupt exit, I couldn't help the smile that crossed my face at the memory of her face planting when Nick burst in.

"I'll make sure it's cleaned up." Dragging my ass off the ground was harder than I first thought. My joints ache after a night on the cold concrete.

I didn't bother to dust myself off as I walked over to the bench, taking another drag of my cigarette before downing the last mouthful of whiskey from the glass I poured before Pepper had arrived.

Arthur was shaking his head when I looked back at him, "Ah to be young," he said with a smile, "If I did that now, I'd be up all night with reflux."

He holds out a coffee to me, eyebrows raised to the now empty tumbler. I accept, mumbling a thanks as I take a deep pull from the foam cup, letting the warmth of the coffee and whiskey warm me from the inside.

We both leaned against the bench, looking back at the sleigh, my dick twitching at the pleasant thoughts it now associated with the red and gold monstrosity.

"You're gonna have to save your cleanup till we get back." Arthur disturbs my thoughts, pulling my concentration back to him.

"Where are we going?" I ask, taking another pull.

"The present wrapping machine has shit itself and Teddy is just about having a coronary, stressing that everything won't get wrapped in time." My lips jerk up in a sly grin at not only Theodore's distress but that our destination is the factory.

Santa's workshop had a much nicer ring to it.

The very same workshop that housed Nick's office.

No time like the present to kick these plans into gear.

I move to grab my tool bag, taking tools off the wall that I thought we might need.

Arthur places his hand on my shoulder, halting my progress. Amusement stains his cheeks, his grin widening as he chuckles under his breath. "You, uh, might wanna go grab a quick shower. You smell like a Swedish Elf brothel."

"Right." I drop the tool bag and down the last of my coffee.

"Is that cum on your shoes?" I choke on my mouthful as he calmly swallows his. My eyes immediately drop to the foot Nick was grinding on, finding nothing there, but my reaction is enough to send Arthur into fits of laughter.

Tossing an oil covered rag off the bench at him, I growl, "Gimme five."

I stalk toward the garage shower, stripping off my overalls and dumping them in the dirty wash basket next to the bathroom.

A wide grin spreads across my face as the water cascades over me and *Operation: Fuck My Big Brother* circles through my mind.

I barely hold back my eye roll as I walk into the factory behind Arthur. Pepper skipping up to greet us both, causes Arthur to give me a knowing wink before he walks towards the machine that needs the repair.

She runs her candy cane decorated nails down my arm, biting her lip. That apparently is my limit though, as I can't hold back the shudder her touch elicits from me, acid burning my throat as my coffee threatens to come back up.

Pepper's eyes narrow at my reaction, but it doesn't deter her from continuing her conversation like I hadn't just almost vomited from her touch.

"Crazy how your brother walked in on us last night, right?" She squeaks, the sound of her voice like nails on a chalkboard, while twisting her fairy floss colored hair around her finger in an attempt to look cute.

"Yeah, crazy."

I wanted to tell her it was even crazier when he dropped to his knees and finished the job she started, only a million times better. I didn't think she would appreciate my commentary though.

Instead, I speed up and lengthen my strides, making her practically have to run to stay by my side. We weave between the hundreds of machines designed to build, process and wrap the toys according to their exact specifications in their Santa letters.

When I first arrived, this was all done by hand, production taking literally all year to process the sheer amount of toys needed for Christmas Day. Now these machines, overseen by the elves, do this in less than half the time. If children sent their letters in late and there was an urgent need for a toy, it worked exceptionally well.

Machines hum all around us, production well underway. The wrapping machine is one of the most important in the line during these final crunch days before Christmas.

Currently, elves grouped in stations at the start of the wrapping machine line were wrapping by hand till we got the machine fixed.

It always surprised me how quickly they could work. A production line of nimble fingers more than capable of any task required to ensure Christmas went ahead no matter what issue may arise.

Though I had plenty of experience with those nimble fingers, none of them held a candle to their boss.

Arthur had already begun work on the machine by the time we arrived. Pepper still hot on my heels, although now she was visibly out of breath, her chest heaving as her hands rested on her hips and she gulped down air.

"So I was thinking maybe tonight," Gasp. Breath, "I could come by after ..." A hopeful grin brightens her face, a flush that might be from the running or her desire, I couldn't tell.

"No." I bark a little too aggressively, cutting her off before she could finish her sentence. Her shoulders deflate and hurt flashes across her face at my refusal.

"I'm swamped with work and Klaus will have my ass if it's not finished on time." It was the wrong thing to say. Leaving the possibility of that door being open in the future perks her right back up.

"Oh yeah, of course." She scuffs her foot on the factory floor, curling her hair again. This time I didn't hold back my eye roll as I took out my tools, laying them on the ground next to Arthur.

"Nothing is more important than Christmas." She said with so much fucking cheer, I have to hold in my grimace. My eyes deadpan and my lips press into a straight line, hoping to hell like I was showing her I was done with this conversation.

When I say nothing, she awkwardly glanced between Arthur and me, then around the room. "Right, so I'll be off. See you around sometime." I mumble a noncommittal hum as she leans up on her toes, lips puckered, waiting for me to lean down and give her a kiss.

The fuck I was. My eyes flick up to the row of glass windows on the second level, at the end of the factory, overlooking the entire work floor. Klaus stands at the window, taking in production from his ivory tower, and next to him is Nick.

With his arms crossed, and a scowl he can't hide, he looks so much like his father when he's mad. Clearly me talking with Pepper was making him so fucking pissed off.

Leaning down, my eyes never drifting from his, I avoid Pepper's mouth instead whispering into her ear

"I have work to do Pepper. Kindly fuck off." Leaning back, I give her my biggest grin, before flicking my gaze back to him.

At this point, I'm surprised that actual smoke isn't coming out of his ears. I knew what my whispering looked like, but part of me knew his jealousy only meant he wanted more of me. That I could get behind.

I shoot him a wink before turning my attention back to the machine and Arthur, who now has half of his body shoved underneath the conveyor belt adjusting some of the internal cogs.

As much as I loved to fuck around and piss off Klaus, I love my job and do it well.

No part of me wanted to ruin Nick's first year as Santa, but the fire that burned hotter in my core as I felt his eyes ghosting over me the entire time I worked, yeah, that was something I wanted more of.

"Good work Son, I hadn't thought of clamping the pipes to those rotators." Arthur claps me on the back as we pack up our tools, sweat glistening across both of our foreheads.

"Yeah, just a lucky guess." I shrug, throwing the last wrench into my bag before zipping it up and tossing it over my shoulder. Running a hand through my hair, I glance up at the windows to see Nick still looking down at us. An idea popping into my head.

"I'm just gonna let Nick know it's done." I yell back to him as I move across the factory floor, not even waiting for his reply.

I practically fly up the stairs to the corporate suites. I could feel the electricity buzzing through my body after being under his intense gaze for the past hour.

Nodding to his receptionist, a blond elf whose name I never bothered to learn, I approached the double door and knocked with my knuckles.

He gruffly replies with a simple "Enter," and a fleeting smile tugs at the corners of my lips before I school my features into a neutral expression. I walk inside, clicking the door shut behind me, relishing in the satisfying sound of the lock engaging. I make sure to leave a greasy hand print on the otherwise pristine white door.

I turn, taking him in. He sits at his desk pretending to be going through paperwork. That scowl is still evident even if lacking the ire of before, but the way he swallows as I move closer, gives away his nervousness at my presence.

I drop my work bag on one of the two chairs set up for guests in front of his glossy red desk, before dropping myself into the other.

I had always hated these offices, each one carrying a different theme. Klaus's is what you would expect from Santa Claus' office: an enormous mahogany desk, red and gold trimmings everywhere, a literal Christmas tree in the corner with fake presents, next to a mammoth fireplace. It wouldn't surprise me if he had found a way to make actual snow fall in his office.

Nick's office has a candy cane theme with white marble floors and red stripes across white walls, which matched his red desk and office chair.

"Do you ever feel like a peppermint threw up in here?" I say, trying to break the tension. It must work as a small smile softens his face, and he lets out a small scoff.

"Every damn day." He lets himself look at me then, a slight blush crossing his cheeks as he takes me in, sweaty from work, covered in grease. Sitting in this pristine office, I couldn't feel more like his opposite.

Scratching at his temple, he fumbles with the paperwork in front of him before giving up and placing both hands firmly on the desk between us. He inhales deeply, icy blue eyes finally looking into mine, body tensing.

"Listen." I cut him off before he has a chance to tell me how much a mistake last night was to him. His words don't mean shit when I've felt his eyes on me for the last hour.

"The machine is working again. You can cancel the ambulance for Theodore's heart attack. It should be running fine now." He relaxes at my quick change of subject.

"Ah, right, thank you. I'll let Dad know." Smiling softly, the lines around his mouth and lips become clearer and my heart clenches at the sight. I feel a desperate need to run my fingers along those smile lines, to memorize every minute detail of his face.

I snap back in my seat, dropping my gaze as I snatch my tool bag and stand. What the fuck was that feeling?

I wanted to fuck him.

That was it.

Right?

It's one thing to have a few hook ups with him, but to feel something more for my stepbrother would be a colossal disaster. The village would erupt. We could literally ruin Christmas.

"Yep, cool. I'll see you around." Though I need to get out, I can't stop myself from taking one last look at him. He looks at me with narrowed eyes, a slight furrow in his brow, trying to read my sudden shift in mood.

He stands as I turn, trying to make a quick exit but barely making it a few steps before his hand stops me.

"Kris, about last night. I'm sorry if what I did made you feel uncomfortable in any way. I just ..." he lets out a sigh, his hands scrubbing at his face. "I just got jealous." My head tilts towards him, his hand still pressed against my forearm. My chest heaves with the restraint it takes to not shove him against the wall and give him everything.

Everything? Is that what I want?

"Of?" I ask.

I know exactly what he was jealous of. I could see it in the factory today, the way he winced every time Pepper touched me, or the scowl that etched itself across his face when she dared to offer a kiss.

"Of ... fuck. Of Pepper, okay?" He lets go of me, turning his back to me as he runs a frustrated hand through his styled salt and pepper hair. The same hair I couldn't get enough of last night, cut to the perfect length so that I could grab handfuls of it to help gain leverage.

My cock stirs in my overalls at the memory of his pouty lips wrapped tight around it, the way his throat gripped me as he gagged on my length. I stare at his back as he rests his hands on his hips, inhaling deeply as he gathers himself.

"I saw her getting you off, and I got jealous." He rushes out the words with a quick exhale, unable to look at me as he speaks. I stand there silently waiting for his confession to tumble free.

"I wanted to be the one getting you off. I wanted to be the one making you white knuckle the sleigh. To push you over the edge."

Exhaling again before turning to face me. "I'm sorry if it wasn't something you wanted,"

"I offered." I shrug.

Nick's brow furrows again as he lets out an exacerbated huff. "I'm still sorry. I should never have barged in on you and Pepper. You're my stepbrother."

He almost looks pained saying those last words. When I remain silent, his desperation to avoid any silence completely consumes him, leading him to incessantly utter the exact words that I have been longing to hear.

"I just couldn't stop myself. I've watched you for so long. Fuck I can't count how many times I've jerked off to the images my brain has created of what you could do to me," Nick whisper yells to avoid being overheard, as his arms wave though the air.

A smirk now tips up the corner of my lips. I've had those thoughts too, every time I caught him staring at my body. There have been times I've been so desperate to touch him, but not wanting to risk fucking up my family, I've kept my distance. That was until he came crashing into my garage.

Now all bets were off the table. Fuck everyone. I wanted him more than I wanted my next breath.

"I just don't want to pressure you into anything you don't want." His shoulder slump with defeat as he sighs.

Dropping my work bag on the floor, deciding I've listened to enough. It was time to make it clear to my big brother just how much I wanted him.

I grab him by the throat and slam him against the wall, making it shudder under our weight. Being the same height was perfect. I didn't have to lean down to push my lips harshly onto his.

His moan fills my mouth, and I take advantage of his gasping mouth to push my tongue in. Claiming him as our tongues lapped against each other, circling, exploring.

This was new for me. I avoided kissing people on the mouth. When I first started fucking people, I tried it but I found it made them get more attached and there were only so many crazy exes a person could live with.

From then on, I avoided it as much as possible, settling for licking and kissing all the other parts of the body, but Nick, I wanted Nick to feel me on his lips when I walked out of those pristine white doors.

I wanted him to crave me.

His hands fist my overalls, and he pulls me closer, tightening the pressure on his throat. I groan into his mouth when his cock tents in his suit pants and brushes against mine, meeting me thrust for thrust as we pant into each other's mouths.

"I'm done hearing you apologize, Nicolas. You know I want you. You knew it last night." Our bodies grind together and I flex my fingers around his throat, pushing his head to the side so I can lick up his jaw, nipping at his ear. "And I sure as hell felt your want today when you stared at Pepper like you wanted her to burst into flames for trying to kiss me."

He tries to answer, but my hand squeezes tighter around his throat, silencing his reply but causing his cock to twitch against mine as his eyes roll back in pleasure.

"I propose we stop denying whatever the hell this is and just roll with it. You want me, and I sure as fuck want you. Let's leave everything else out of it and let me make you feel like a fucking god." I offer as his eyes widen and he nods as much as he can while still pinned to the wall. My free hand lowers to unbuckle his suit pants, pulling them and his boxers down his thighs enough so his dick can spring free.

Damn, I knew he was packing, but two of my hands would have a hard time covering his length. The feel of his silky thickness against my calloused hand as I run up and down has me wanting to press bruising kisses to his lips.

Nick gasps into my waiting mouth as my hand continues to pump. My thumb pausing to swipe the precum from his tip.

After rubbing it in circles over the slit, I bring my thumb to my mouth, swiping my tongue across the pad. My eyes fall shut at the salty taste on my tongue and I moan. When I open my eyes, the blue of his eyes are nearly gone, pupils blown wide, glued to the movement.

I release the pressure on his neck and he gasps for air, sucking in gulps as my hand continues to move back and forth against his length. He can't stop his hips from pumping into my hand as he pants with need, thrusting, leaning forward, trying to claim my lips.

"Kris," He hisses as his head falls back against the wall, "I'm coming."

Releasing my grip on him, I drop to my knees. Taking a second to admire his impressive cock this close to my face, I grin up at him, winking, as his eyes widen in shock before covering his dick with my mouth and slamming it straight to the back of my throat.

Gripping my hair, he cries my name as he continues grinding into me. My hands grip onto his ass, the muscles clenching in my hands as he spills warm, salty cum deep into my throat and I groan around him.

Fuck, I have never been so turned on.

A knock at the door startles us, my mouth popping off as Nick fumbles for his suit pants. I stand, shoving him back against the wall, my body flush with his, my aching cock pressing against his stomach. His wide eyes shift between me and the door, panic covering his face.

He pauses when I open my mouth, showing him the cum covering my tongue, his mouth gapes before he swallows and licks his lips.

Good boy.

With his attention pinned on me, I slowly run my hand up the side of his face, fingers raking through the base of his hair, loving the way he mewls at my touch and crush our lips back together for one last claiming kiss.

Our tongues swirl, a mixture of saliva and cum coating us both. Together, we groan and ignore the persistent knocking at his door.

Releasing him from the kiss, our foreheads rest together as we both pant in each other's arms.

I let him go when Klaus' voice booms through the door, "Nick?"

Stepping back, I pick up my bag from where I dropped it, throwing it over my shoulder before pulling the cigarette pack out of my pocket. After I place it in my mouth, I adjust my cock in my overalls so it isn't obvious to everyone outside how fucking hard I am.

Though if I was honest, I wasn't one hundred percent sure if I cared anymore.

Placing my hand on the door, I took one last look back at Nick as he leans against the wall, still trying to catch his breath. I soak in his just fucked appearance, the rosy tint covering his cheeks and the tip of his nose, his rumpled suit and hair.

"If you want more, you know where to find me."

Flicking the lock with one hand, I wink before swinging the door wide.

"Should be alright now, Nick," I say over my shoulder, looking at Klaus standing in the doorway, brow furrowed as he looks between us. I revel in the taste of his son, still on the forefront of my taste buds.

"What's up Klaus?" I ask, cigarette bouncing in between my lips. "Catch you later Nick."

A small sound of acknowledgment seems to be all he can get out before coughing and turning back to his desk.

Once in the elevator, I turn to lean back on the railing. I can still see Klaus staring at me from Nick's doorway. I can't help but shoot him a wink and salute as the doors close.

My grin is abnormally wide as I make my way back to the garage.

I am abso-fucking-lutely gonna fuck my stepbrother.

CHAPTER FIVE

Nick

FOLLOWING AN UNCOMFORTABLE CONVERSATION with my father regarding Kris being in my office with the door locked, he dumped a massive pile of new scrolls on my desk. He then proceeded to spend twelve hours meticulously explaining the contents of each list.

I hoped to God that my story about him being here to fix my lock sounded convincing enough.

Finally alone, I stare at the mountain of paperwork I need to sort through. Naughty and nice lists that need double checking, inventory of every present request and what we could and couldn't deliver this year. The lists, quite frankly, are overwhelming.

Maybe the Toy Development Elves could come up with a computer program that could streamline it all, making list checking much more efficient, because a hand written thirty-five foot long parchment was not the way of the future.

Groaning, I flop myself into my chair; swiveling to get a better view of the workshop. It's hard to believe in three days this place will officially be mine.

My chest tightens at the responsibility now looming on my shoulders. Two billion children will need me to be on top of my game all year round.

Even though it was getting well into the night, by December, the workshop was on a twenty-four hour rotation.

There were no repeats. Each toy was one of a kind.

Quality Control Elves ensured that each toy that came out was perfectly tailored to each child's request. If there was an issue, they sent it back to the smelter to be destroyed and recycled, then recreated the toy.

The long line of Claus' had perfected the tedious process over generations, ensuring that every child in the world woke up to their dream gift under the tree.

Turning back to my desk, I sigh as I take in the mammoth amount of work in front of me.

Running a finger over my lips, I smile at the way they tingle after Kris' possessing kisses. His cum filled kiss was the single hottest thing I've ever felt in my life, second only to him on his knees, mouth worshiping my cock.

I let out a small growl at the parchments covering my desk as I look out the external window of my office. This window overlooks the entire village square.

People were making their way home as the night grew darker, but my gaze landed on the snow covered metal garage that housed not only the sleigh, but someone who was quickly becoming the most important person in my life.

I had expected him to brush our hookup from last night off as just that, a hookup, laughing at me as he flipped me off, walking out of my office.

Pinning me up against the wall and shoving his hand into my pants, dropping to his knees in front of me to give me the best orgasm of my life, or kissing me with my cum still warm in his mouth had definitely not been on my BINGO card of how the morning was going to go.

The side window of the shed glows through the frost clouding over the glass, letting me know he is still there, still waiting for me.

Hidden away in the bottom drawer, the aged bottle of scotch my father had thoughtfully chosen for my thirtieth birthday seemed to whisper promises of relaxation and indulgence. Giving in, I pull it out and pour myself a more than generous amount and knock it back in a single satisfying mouthful.

I knew what would happen if I went to him. God, did I want to feel him again, touch him, fuck him, but these fucking papers were too important to skip out on.

I allow myself one more look out the window, promising myself that if that light was still on when I finished, I would go to him.

Kris's cock being the best incentive I could dream of, I grab my pen and set to work, ensuring that all children were marked into their correct lists.

The next time I look up, the clock on the far wall of my office reads two a.m. Rubbing at my eyes, I dare another glance out the window, holding my breath as my eyes narrow in on the garage.

The soft, glowing light continued to shine brightly like a beacon.

My smile widens, and I push myself out of my seat, quickening my steps as I move towards the door. Pausing only to wrap my coat and scarf around me, I practically run through the empty office to the elevator, punching the down button, silently urging the doors to shut faster.

My stomach flutters with nerves, foot tapping as I glare at the numbers, slowly counting down.

As I leave the building, I make a conscious effort to slow down and bid good night to the night workers, restraining myself from dashing to the garage like a lovesick teen.

Though if I was honest with myself, I hadn't ever been this excited to see someone.

I wipe my sweaty, trembling hands on my coat, then tuck them into my pockets as I approach the side door, making sure no one would notice me entering. Although knowing that anyone that saw me would never guess my true purpose for being here, I couldn't help but feel a surge of excitement.

I attempt to knock on the door before mentally slapping myself because I still had my hands shoved in my pockets. Self doubt creeps in and I pause as I raise my hand inches from the door.

What were we doing? This could destroy not only our entire family, but our community. I hated to admit that Santa's village wasn't very open about different sexualities, not to mention the expectation that I would marry a nice girl and carry on our family's traditions.

I knew I didn't want a nice girl though. I want the man on the other side of that metal door with his cocky grin, covered in grease, who smelled like tobacco and mint.

With my decision made, my knuckles knock but the door pulls open before I have a chance. Warmth from the garage hits me in the face, melting the small dusting of snow that had gathered on my eyelashes from the short walk here.

Kris stands there, wiping those strong, calloused hands on an oil stained rag, smirking at me, his cigarette dangling from the side of his mouth.

"Are you just gonna stand there, or are you coming in?" His dark eyebrow quirks as his jade eyes shine with mischief, and I nod eagerly as I step in.

The sound of the door closing echoes in my ears, and suddenly my mouth feels dry, my ability to speak slipping away. I can't tear my eyes away from his hands, the same hands that had given me pleasure earlier, now flexing around the lock.

He returns to his workbench, abandoning the rag, and I steal a moment to divert my gaze from his muscular frame hidden beneath the dark gray coveralls to the enormous sleigh before me.

At least sixty feet of intimidating red and glittering gold, look back at me. My face tightens, lips pressing into a flat line as I make hesitant steps towards the extravagant monstrosity that represents the epitome of my family legacy.

Although the outside shell looks the same as it did when the original Santa Claus, my great-great-great-great grandfather first took to the skies. The inside—thanks to Kris—has had a total overhaul. Their dream to bring the sleigh into the modern era, becoming a reality.

Dials, knobs and screens now fill the dashboard. State-of-the-art guidance systems, radar navigation and stardust amplifiers allowed for ease of use and helped make the sleigh as efficient as possible.

Kris was currently working on specially designed helmets for the reindeer, which allowed for real time directional changes directly to the cockpit based on potential hazards or delays.

My personal favorite was the hot cocoa dispenser Kris added into the center console last Christmas. Before that, my father had cup trays filled with thermoses which would usually run out somewhere over North America.

My head spins with the realization that in just a few days, I will take the reins, literally, and I brace myself on the lip of the cockpit door to steady the dizzying thoughts.

The list of jobs to complete within that time flooding my brain. Checking inventory, route preparation, last-minute suit alterations ... A warm body presses into my back and I instantly feel myself relax. Preparation concerns becoming snowflakes on the breeze.

Kris' breath tickles the shell of my ear as he leans over me, pushing my body into the titanium shell. The smell of freshly polished leather mixes with Kris' scent and I have to bite my lip to hold in the moan, already wanting to slip past my lips.

"Do you like the new upgrades?" he purrs next to my ear.

Words feel like lacquer in my throat as I try to think of something cool to say back to him.

"It ah, looks shinier?" I cringe, *'shinier'*. Seriously, what the fuck is wrong with me?

My voice breaks and I sound like, now at thirty-one, my balls are just finally dropping and I mentally face palm myself.

Of course, I know about the new upgrades to the sleigh. We had meetings about the major titanium upgrades to the runners back in January. It had been one of the first projects that my father had actually let Kris lead.

How have I already fucked this up in the first sentence I've said to him tonight? I just can't manage to form coherent sentences with his body pressed up against mine, and his rock hard length rubbing against my ass.

I brace for the coolness to hit my back as he leaves, deciding he is done with me. A huff of warm air brushes against the back of my neck, but he doesn't move away.

His hand skims across my hip to brace against the sleigh. The other brushes passed mine, and he points to the new dials added to the dash. I shiver as he surrounds me, loving the feeling of being boxed in by his muscular arms.

"This one is the updated stardust equalizer." I hum in response as his breath whispers over my ear, closing my eyes as I feel him smirk against my shoulder.

"What does that do?" I feel like I should remember this, but right now, with Kris pressed so tightly against my body, all knowledge slips from my brain. My only thoughts are how he tastes and how good it felt to explode into his mouth. How desperate I am to do it again. To do more.

"It stabilizes the amount of stardust emanating from the sleigh so you don't end up overtaking the reindeer."

The sleigh used to rely solely on reindeer magic, but as belief in Santa Claus wanes, we've had to find alternative sources. Stardust.

The level of stardust input had to be altered by my father, mid-flight, depending on the flight requirements, either increasing or decreasing it. It was a delicate balance.

Too much stardust and like Kris said, the sleigh would overtake the reindeer. Too little, and it adds too much pressure on the reindeer, risking burnout. Kris' latest upgrade should hopefully make this less of an issue that I will need to focus on throughout my flight.

"Yeah, that would ... umm ... be bad." I'm a fucking moron.

Another huff of a laugh brushes across my ear. "Yes, Santa. That would be bad." The way he drags out the name Santa like he is testing how it feels as it rolls across his tongue has me biting the inside of my cheek, feeling flush.

"Did you have a productive afternoon?" he asks.

Now it's my turn to scoff. Productive is not what I would call it.

"I had to sit through hours of meetings with my father."

"And that wasn't productive?" his mouth moves to my other ear and I shiver at the contact of his teeth grazing my ear.

"Not when all I could think about was how hot you looked with my cock in your mouth."

This time his tongue licks a path up my neck, his hot breath eliciting a moan from deep in my chest as I press back into him, locked between him and the sleigh.

"So you've been thinking about my cock all day?" He punctuates his question with the press of his hard erection against my ass and I whimper.

"Use your words, Santa Baby," he growls.

Slowly, he grinds against me. My rock hard cock presses against the cool titanium sides of the cockpit. The thin material of my trousers the only thing stopping me from fucking the side of the sleigh.

"Yes," I stutter out, "all day." I moan as he grinds against me again.

"Good, because the sweet taste of you has lingered in my mouth all day," he says as he places a kiss against the base of my neck. "Do you know how hard it is to get my work done when my dick has been aching for you all day?"

Oh, I know. I've had to subtly readjust my pants as my arousal reignited with each glance at the wall in my office.

When I'm unable to answer, the contrast of the flush of my skin and the cool titanium too much, he continues. "I've spent my day bent over this cockpit, imagining how good you are going to feel when I get inside of you. How warm and inviting your ass will be. How tightly you will clamp down on my cock as you beg me to fuck you harder."

With another grind, I'm lost. It's like I can't breathe.

"Please," I whisper, the word barely coming out.

"Please what?" The command in his voice making me subconsciously grind myself back against him.

"Please Kris." I gasp for air as his hand moves down my waist. "I want you to fuck me."

I'm pretty sure I've wanted this longer than I have let myself admit.

His heat disappears as he steps back and I almost collapse at the lack of contact. Turning, I see him walking back to his workbench, sliding open a drawer at the back of his toolbox and pulling out something I can't see.

The boyish grin he gives me as he leans against the bench is one I will never forget. He props the bottle of lube on the table next to him, his arms crossing over his chest, looking the epitome of casual. Like he has all the time in the world for me.

"Strip." I blink at his request, and his eyebrow quirks as he waits for my decision.

I try to hide the shake in my hands as I raise them to remove my tie. It flutters to the floor as my hands move back to the buttons of my shirt, one I've worn many times, now feels too constricting, suffocating.

As it falls open, my hands move to my belt buckle. My eyes don't stray from Kris as he watches, unmoving.

Unbuckling my belt, I pop the button on my pants, allowing it to gape. I'm not self-conscious, but I am very aware that my body looks nothing like his.

In my family, the Santa genes are unmistakable. Premature white hair, rosy cheeks, and a soft rounded stomach. But when Kris' eyes darken at the sight of me, it's as if none of those traits matter anymore.

Eyes twinkling, he looks like a child getting his first glimpse of a tree full of presents on Christmas morning. He licks his lips and I feel like I am the gift he has been waiting all year for. He is relishing in my unwrapping. Savoring it.

I kick off my shoes and trousers into a pile next to me, looking back at him for his next command. His eyes rake over my body, hot and wanting as he takes in every dip and curve.

He stares back into my eyes as he slowly lowers the zip to his coveralls, the tip of his erection peeking through the gap once it's fully undone.

Heat pools in my stomach and I feel my cock jerk. The movement pulling Kris' gaze instantly, that smirk returning.

After slipping his arms out, the material slides easily down his body, pooling on the floor. Kris takes the time to undo his laces and remove his boots before kicking the outfit out of the way.

Without another glance, he disappears into a side room. I stand naked in the middle of his workspace, my cock jutting out in front of me, not sure what I'm meant to do.

Just when I'm starting to think he has left me here to be discovered by God knows who, he reappears, a loop of Christmas Lights draped over his shoulder and a mischievous gleam in his eyes.

Walking over to the sleigh, he snatches the bottle of lube on his way past the bench before disappearing behind the sleigh. A scraping noise on the concrete has goosebumps pebbling over my flesh and I try to stretch to see what he is doing, jolting back into my position as he stands up.

Once he is on the side of the sleigh, he casually leans against the leather seats, like he hasn't just ordered me to strip and left me in the middle of the room.

With his eyes tracing every inch of my bare skin, I instinctively hold my breath, anticipating his next move. Crossing his arms over his chest, his smirk drops, eyes darkening.

"Crawl to me." I just about choke on the lack of air, but my body responds to his demand. Dropping to my knees before slowly bending to rest my weight onto my palms, never taking my eyes off his.

His muscles contract, his body stiffening as his eyes remain fixated on me. Slowly, I edge forward, crawling across the dirty concrete to where he waits.

When I reach him, I sit back on my knees and wait. My body is humming with the anticipation of his next request.

He circles me like a predator toying with his prey, knowing he has already won.

Behind me, he stops. I feel his breath hot against my ear as he presses a lingering kiss to the spot behind my ear, my eyes closing.

"Climb into the cockpit. Same position." His fingers rake through my curls before he steps back.

I hesitate for a second in front of the sleigh, thoughts flashing through my brain of fucking inside what is basically a family heirloom, but the heat of his body behind me melts away any doubts I have.

The cold leather bites into my knees as I kneel on the bench seat facing the back of the sleigh. As I lower into the position, my balls press into the seat and I bite my lip to hold in the moan that the friction elicits. My muscles feel so tense with the buildup, I feel like I'm a slight breeze away from a big problem.

The sleigh dips as Kris climbs in after me, and I look over my shoulder to watch him. Pulling the looped lights off his shoulder, he tilts his head, eyes dipping down to take an appreciative look at my ass in this new position.

When he sees me watching, his smirk comes back. Unraveling the lights, he lets the excess fall to his feet.

"If you want this to stop, we stop. At any point." I stare at him with wide eyes.

What does he mean?

I haven't been able to stop my imagination running wild with thoughts of how he is going to feel pushing inside me since he walked out of my office.

His face softens as he takes in my confusion.

"If anything I do makes you uncomfortable, you say the word, and it stops. Okay?" His gentleness takes me by surprise and I nod, probably looking like one of the reindeer when one of the snow mobiles gets too close.

"I need words, Santa baby,"

"I understand." With a slight curl of his lips, he grips my chin and pulls me in for a toe-curling kiss. As he breaks away, his teeth playfully nip at my bottom lip.

"Hands behind your back." he orders.

I comply, locking my wrists together behind my body. He expertly weaves the lights around my hands, locking them together. A flat palm on the center of my back has my chest pressed over the top of the bench, and I am spread wide for him. Feeling the most exposed I have ever felt with another person, woman or man.

His groan has my ass clenching and the snick of the cap is the only warning I have before cool liquid runs between my cheeks. I gasp when a finger catches the drip, running it up and down the seam, lingering over my hole a little longer with each pass.

I try to stare over my shoulder to watch what he is doing, but the lights make it hard to twist myself enough to see. I can only manage to see his face as he stares, entranced as his finger circles my puckered entrance, tongue darting out to run along the seam of his lips.

"Fuck," I groan as his finger presses in and his eyes briefly flash up to my face, taking in my expression before they snap back to his finger as he moves deeper. I feel my muscles tense refusing the intrusion but he gently shushes me, massaging my tense cheeks with the hand not currently dipping in my asshole.

"Breathe baby, you're doing so well."

His withdrawal has me whimpering, the emptiness now feeling unbearable.

"Please…"

I push back, offering my ass to him, and beg for more.

More cool liquid drips over my hole and his finger as he presses in, firmer this time. I wince, but the back and forth is becoming easier. He circles, rubbing his finger along my inner walls, hitting a spot that makes my forehead drop to the bench. The feeling is too good to waste strength holding my head up.

"Yes, that's it, baby. Are you ready for more?"

I think I nod, but I'm lost in the motions and his movement. This time, when he withdraws, he adds an extra finger. Both digits fill me in a way I could never have imagined. I haven't even touched my cock, but I can feel the impending release building.

His fingers spread, scissoring in me, preparing me.

"Fuck, my cock is dying to fuck this ass. God, you're perfect."

I raise my head, our eyes locking and I beg "Do it. Fuck my ass."

His mouth drops in an 'O' before snapping shut, his smirk returning. He positions himself behind me, the sound of the lube squelching as he drips it into his hand. With deliberate, unhurried movements, he strokes his dick, coating it in a glossy sheen.

The head of his length rubs against my hole, the same way his finger started as I mimic the movements, desperate to feel him inside me.

"Deep breath baby. This is a lot bigger than my fingers." I breathe in, anticipation making my legs shake. As I exhale, he slides himself inside me and I wince at the intrusion but groan as his cock rubs me in a way no other has.

"FUCK!" He groans, his voice sounds huskier than I've ever heard it. He's not even fully seated, just pulsing half way and I know I will never get enough.

He slowly draws back, pushing slightly deeper when he returns, and I grind my hardness against the leather, desperate for more friction. The leather bench is hot and sticky underneath my skin, and provides just the right amount of friction I need. That paired with Kris' thrusts, I'm quickly being dragged closer and closer to oblivion.

As he sits himself fully inside me, he pauses, hand gently stroking up my spine, voice sounding enamored, "I knew I'd fit. Fuck baby, you were made for me."

His words make my stomach clench as the butterflies that permanently reside there whenever he is near take flight. I cry out his name as my orgasm rockets through my body. My whole body comes to life with his touch and his words.

"That's it baby. Come for me while I'm buried so deep in your ass."

Hot cum spurts from my cock, covering my stomach and the leather, dripping between my legs into a puddle underneath me.

Kris groans behind me, legs shaking as his release fills my hole. His hands flex on my hips, gripping me tighter as he rides the waves of his orgasm. He stays tights against my body till the pulsing dulls, unlike the beating of my heart.

I pant, collapsing against the seat, no strength left to hold myself up. Kris' body presses against mine as he lies on top of me, pressing a soft kiss to my shoulder.

His body shakes, a chuckle rising deep within him. I lift my head, raising my eyebrows in question, confused by his sudden case of the giggles.

"I just thought of what I want for Christmas?"

"What?"

The boyish grin that splits his face, hair falling across his eyes as he looks at me, has my heart doing cartwheels.

"More lube." he says bursting out laughing, "Buckets and buckets of it."

A smile curls at my lips as I dip my head back against his chest. "Well, have you been naughty or nice?"

His eyes darken as his hand wraps around my throat, flexing his long fingers as he tightens his hold, lips brush against mine.

"Naughty, definitely naughty."

Chapter Six

Nick

I FEEL COCOONED IN a layer of warmth, like being curled up next to a roaring fire while a blizzard rages outside. Contentment like I've never experienced fills me as thoughts of last night and the hours that followed flood my memory.

The sleigh is still spacious despite both of our six foot frames filling the back tray. In two days time, we will fill this section with the bottomless present receptacle. For now though, the metal tray remains empty, except for our entwined bodies and the scrappy blanket Kris draped over the cool metal surface as we collapsed, exhausted and satiated just before morning.

Kris' warm chest lifts against my cheek as he wakes with a stretch. Lifting my head, I drink him in. Mussed hair looking hot as hell even as it sticks up at odd angles, hazy green eyes meet mine and a lazy grin stretches across his face before he rubs the sleep from his eyes.

"What time is it?" I ask and he leans to the side to see the giant red clock on the wall of the garage, still holding my body close to his.

"Just after six." Not that the time really mattered. Sunrise isn't a thing here during winter. We spend months of the year in the dark. "Good morning," he greets me, voice gravelly and laced with sleep. His eyes drop to my lips, his tongue darts out to run over his bottom lip.

As I lay close to his face, I notice his eyes, a mesmerizing shade of jade, speckled with hints of gold. They shimmer with the reflections of the lamplight streaming through the garage window.

His hand gently touches my bare arm, rubbing his thumb in small circles against my skin.

Moving his face closer to mine, he hesitates before our lips touch, seemingly unsure of his next move, a side I haven't seen of him yet. I've seen angry Kris, cocky Kris, dominating Kris, even a gentle Kris when he is alone with his mom, but I have never seen him look unsure of himself.

"Good morning." With a simple gesture of tilting my chin, I offer myself to him, and he wastes no time in accepting. His hand tenderly cups my cheek as he presses his lips against mine in a gentle, unhurried kiss. It's a stark contrast to the fiery passion that consumed us the previous night.

No, this kiss has the ability to change me at my core, my heart constricting as we sit suspended in this moment together.

Our lips linger together, exploring, branding. My hands learn the dips and curves of his muscles as they clench under my touch, stopping when they find his chest. I run my fingers through the sporadic hair finding their way to one pebbled nipple. When I squeeze it gently, he groans into my mouth. Our bare chests press together as we shuffle closer.

I should leave. There are still so many preparations for the biggest day of my life, but I can't pull myself away. Against his body, I feel like I am exactly where I am supposed to be.

Kris' kisses become more desperate. He easily takes control and I am happy to follow his lead. He leans over me, slowly pushing me onto his back before hovering over my body.

My semi-hard cock now stands at attention as the tip brushes his abs before his length rubs against my own. I gasp at the sensation, Kris' mouth devouring the noise before he slowly grinds against me again.

"I need to be in that ass again." His gruff voice in my ear has me bucking against his cock as he grinds his erection along my shaft. "Are you too sore?"

I shake my head vehemently, needing to feel him inside me again. Part of me had worried that I would wake up this morning and all of this would be a dream. That I hadn't spent the most incredible night with the man that has been a constant feature in my fantasies.

He growls before leaning back onto his knees, reaching for the bottle of lube. I'm almost surprised it isn't empty after the amount we used last night.

I just about come on the spot, watching him squirt a large dollop into his hand before running up the length of his shaft in one firm swipe, squeezing the tip, his gaze darkening as my cock bobs against my stomach, waiting for him.

His glistening finger finds my entrance and I moan as his finger runs around the outside, teasing me before the tip presses in, my head bangs against the metal tray as it drops back.

Fuck. Even after all the stretching and care he took last night, I'm sore, but fuck does it still feel good.

"Fuck. Your ass is begging for me," he growls as he presses his finger in further, my cock bouncing towards him in a desperate attempt for him to touch. "I'm going to make it so this ass remembers who it belongs to."

"Oh, God." I groan as he pulls back, suddenly feeling empty before his fingers are back, pushing into my entrance. The extra pressure is overwhelming, "Please Kris. Fuck me."

A dark chuckle is his response as he pushes them in, gently scissoring to spread me further, just like he did last night. "Oh, Santa baby. I want to worship this ass, not destroy it. I have my own naughty list I plan to work through, this is only the beginning."

My dick weeps with his promises. I don't know what the future has in store for us, but I would be happy to live in the back of this sleigh with him forever.

When he is satisfied I'm primed enough, he shuffles closer. He lifts my knees over his toned thighs, placing himself tightly in between my legs. I shudder in anticipation as he massages his cock, lining it up with my entrance.

He stares, mesmerized at the sight as he slowly pushes into me. He pauses, his chest is heaving as my tight hole clenches around the intrusion. I whimper at the feeling, wiggling my ass to get him to move further inside me, growing impatient at his pace.

"Nick," he warns, the tone sending a lightning bolt straight to my dick, now angry and red, pulsing, which catches his attention. "If your ass wiggles on my cock again, I will flip you over and pound the shit out of you."

I know it's not the time, but I can't help the snort that comes out, "Don't threaten me with a good time."

His eyebrow cocks and I regret my choice of words as he drives in hard and fast, not giving me time to adjust before sinking to the hilt. I gasp at his sudden intrusion, the burn as he stretches me beyond my limits.

"Oh, fuck." Precum leaks over my stomach each time my cock rubs against my skin.

"Not so cocky now, are we?" His lips tip up, knowing he has proved his point, and he eases up, gliding more gently inside me. "Are you ready to be a good boy?" I nod at a loss for words, the pulse in my core overriding the burn.

I need him.I need him to move. I am desperate for him to stroke my cock.

"Kris please," I whimper and he pulls back, leaving just the head inside me. I feel empty and needy. Eager for more. I can't get over how good this feels.

His dick teases my hole as he reaches for my aching shaft, wrapping a firm hand around it, I moan as he pushes back inside me. The feeling of being stretched and stroked at the same time is overwhelming.

He throws his head back in pleasure as he lets out a long groan. His eyes squeeze shut as he grinds into me while jerking me at the same time.

"Good morning, Glenda. How are the kids this morning?"

We both freeze at the deep rumble of my father's voice outside the garage, my eyes going wide as I realize the scene he is about to walk into.

Kris slowly pulls out of me and even though I know we can't continue, I still whimper at the loss.

"...yes, just popping in on Kris to check how the sleigh is going." Kris' mother responds to an unheard question and that is the jolt we need to spring into action.

Kris jumps out of the sleigh first, hard cock bobbing against his stomach as his feet hit the ground with a gentle thud. He reaches for his coveralls, not bothering to grab his boxers that lay strewn on the other side of the room as he slides them on.

I follow suit, jumping out and racing around the room, trying to collect my items of clothes that somehow seem to be spread all over the place.

Kris grins as I scramble, casually zipping up his coveralls, leaving his chest exposed as he tries to hold back a laugh.

"I can't find my pants!" I whisper yell at him, not wanting our parents to overhear us.

"Did you lose them before or after the candy cane?" He offers as help, pulling out a cigarette from his pocket, fighting with the crumpled packet as he leans casually back against the sleigh we have just spent eight hours fucking in.

I pause my stalking to glare at him. "Seriously?"

He shrugs, lighting his smoke, as if it's a valid question. Last night is burned into my brain and at the same time a total fucking blur. Years worth of fantasies rolled into one and even though I am seconds away from being caught, literally with my pants down in my stepbrother's garage, I can't bring myself to regret any of it.

"What the fuck am I going to wear?" My voice rising to an almost hysterical whisper with my panic.

He stands straight, cigarette poised between his lips as he glances around the space. He strides towards a rack in the corner. He pulls some deep red material from the shelf before walking it over to the bench. Pulling a pocket knife out from the draw, he slices two cuts in the material, turning to proudly present it to me.

I take it from his outstretched hand, handing him the half of my ensemble I could find. Holding the edge, I let the material drop to the floor.

"You have got to be joking." I look back at him, disbelief clear on my face.

"It was the best I could do with short notice." Another shrug, but a small smirk tickles the edge of his lips, the fucker taking pleasure from my panic.

I look back down at the vintage present bag. At one stage it was probably filled with toys for children riding on the back of my grandfather's sleigh. It's redundant now because of our present receptacle upgrades. Regardless, it definitely wasn't meant to be worn.

The clattering of the doorknob has me sprinting into action. "Fuck it," I mumble quickly threading one leg in after the other and hauling the bag up over my body, repressing a shudder at the fact I look like I'm wearing an over-sized diaper.

Kris hands back what we could find of my clothing, before leaning forward and gripping my chin, pulling me in for one last dominating kiss before he lets me go, nodding towards the side door.

"If you don't want to say hi to Mom and Dad on the way out, that way is probably safer." He steps towards the main doors, opening it to greet our parents as I make my escape along the side of the house.

The snow is freezing against my feet, but I sneak to the front of the building just to double check they haven't worked out Kris wasn't alone.

"Oh Kris," Carol's cheerful voice rings across the thankfully still empty village center. Glenda must have been heading home after being at the bakery through the night. "I didn't realize we were interrupting you." She coughs, uncomfortable.

"It's fine, my guest just left." Kris' gruff voice, laced with a hint of annoyance at our interruption.

"Who is the lucky elf?" My father croons but Kris refuses to respond, simply glaring at him before taking another drag of his cigarette and tossing it into the snow at his feet.

"We were just wanting to check how you were going and invite you to breakfast." She nudges my father, and he coughs before agreeing with her invitation.

"Yeah, I just have a few more tweaks of the reindeer hazard alert units and they should be ready for their test flight in a few hours."

Kris asks if they want to see the new helmets, my father hums his agreement and Kris holds the door open for them. I slip around the side as they disappear inside.

I steal one last glance as Kris standing there looking just fucked, his hair disheveled and a rosy glow brightens his cheeks as he leans against the open door.

He gives me a quick wink, and my eyes drop to the tent in his coveralls. A blush creeping up my cheeks causes him to smirk and I shake my head.

As the garage door shuts behind him, I double check the coast is clear before running for my house, clothing bundled in my hands attempting to hold up my giant diaper pants.

Sharp pain shoots up my feet, my toes already bright red from the cold. Any longer and I'll be in big trouble.

I take the stairs two at a time, trying not to trip on the sagging material. I shiver as I open the front door and the warmth hits my skin.

I make it up to the bathroom, turning on the shower to a lukewarm, slowly warming my feet up. When I can feel the circulation returning to my toes, I turn the water up warmer and step under the spray.

I sigh as the warmth seeps into my aching muscles. After a night of sleeping on a hard sleigh bed, and the best sex I've ever had, my body is sorer than I realized.

Of all the thoughts that should run through my head this close to Christmas, the only thing I can think of is that I can't wait to fuck my stepbrother again.

Chapter Seven

Kris

"Fuck!" I spit out, slamming my soldering iron onto the workbench. The candles burn down to stubs at my station as it gets later into the evening.

I can't get this relay to work properly. Without this connection, the signal won't transmit properly to the sleigh, leaving the reindeer unable to relay any incoming hazards.

After spending the last six months on this project, now was crunch time. Klaus had trusted me to oversee this upgrade, and with just two days left it needs to be up and running with zero glitches, and I still can't get a basic connection to work seamlessly.

Maybe Klaus was right, and I didn't belong here. The idea of leaving used to bring me comfort. That if worst came to worst, I could say fuck it and walk away.

Leaving my mother would be hard, but through all of his faults, Klaus was a good husband. Shitty stepfather, but he loved my mother with everything he was.

Now the idea of leaving the village and trying to set up a home somewhere new brought memories of twinkling blue eyes and the way salt and pepper stubble felt against my skin.

Pushing the metal shield off my face, leaving it to rest on top of my head, I grab my half empty water bottle and drain it in a single mouthful before throwing it in the trash can next to me.

The multi-colored lights flash over my head and I press the heels of my hands into my eyes. I need to get this to work.

A warm hand rests on my shoulder, causing me to tense, my hand curling into a fist. "Sometimes when I'm stuck, it helps to walk away and come back to it later." Arthur's husky voice sweeps over me, and I relax.

His pipe sits lopsided in his mouth as he grins at me. The wafting smell of cloves and tobacco surrounds me and the familiarity comforts me.

Arthur has been smoking the same tobacco mix out of the same Briarwood pipe since I arrived at the village. I once joked that he would smoke a hole through the pipe one day, but he insists it only gets better with age.

He straddles the gas lift stool next to me, resting his foot on the lever and gently pressing down, raising himself to sit eye level with me.

"You seem different, distracted even?" His mouth puffs around the mouthpiece and a plume of smoke winds up towards the vaulted ceilings.

I shrug, not really knowing how to tell the man that has been there for me every day for the last twelve years that I've spent the last two days fucking the brains out of my stepbrother. The man that in two days will take over the reins, literally, of this entire operation.

How can I tell him that over those past two days, it went from exploring an interest in Nick that I've harbored for the last sixteen years to something that makes my heart grow. That maybe my mind believes I may still want a future in this festive frenzy of a village?

"Does this have anything to do with your late nights at the shop?" His eyes assess me.

"I've been trying to get this damn sleigh to not crash at the first hazard Nick comes across." I bite out, turning back to my soldering, not wanting him to see the truth.

"Then why haven't you asked me to stay back with you?" His eyes glimmer with mischief and he knows he has got me when my cheeks flush and he hums his victory. "That's what I thought."

I huff a response before smacking down my mask so I don't need to look at his satisfied grin. I pick up my soldering iron.

"This one means something?" His question lacks any hint of judgment. From the moment I walked through those doors at seventeen, his knack for deciphering my thoughts without me saying a word has been a curse.

Through the visor of the metal shield, I can almost see concern cross his features and my brows draw together at his worry.

Is it for me, or for what I might do? Does he think I'm not capable of developing feelings for someone?

I tighten my fists and he glances at my hands, his eyes narrowing slightly before he places his hand on my shoulder once more.

"Son." I pause at the sentiment, my face softening at the gentleness of his expression, before lifting my mask back off my face.

"I hope you know I am proud of you," he whispers, his eyes shining. "I know I am not your father, but it has been a great joy in mine and Mary Lou's life watching you grow into the capable man you are today."

I hold my breath at the mention of his wife. Arthur rarely mentions her since she passed two winters ago, but now and then I catch him staring at the photo of her he has tucked into his wallet. He doesn't wait for me to speak as he continues. "I hope that whoever they are, they recognize the potential your heart has for love. Even if you hide it behind that cocky grin and what you believe to be a tough exterior."

"Nick ..." Is all I get out before he nods, perceptively and reassuringly pats my shoulder.

"Well, that is tough, but no one said love was supposed to be easy."

"Love? Oh no, it's not ..." I splutter, sitting up straight, nearly knocking the reindeer helmet off the bench in my haste to deny.

"It's okay son. It might not be yet, but I have seen the way you two have danced around each other over the years."

I open my mouth to protest, but my shoulders slump as his observation hits me. "What? You have?"

"Of course, I would need to be blind to not see it. Even my Mary Lou used to comment on how well you two would complement each other. Opposites attract and what not." He waves off dramatically as he puffs clouds of white smoke around us.

"But what about him being my stepbrother?" I question, torn between a sliver of hope at a future and the weight of this question.

"Is it an issue for you?" He asks indignantly, the directness of his question taking me by surprise.

Thinking back to how excited I was at the prospect of touching him, how much I've thought about his hot mouth on me, how now, after such a short time, this doesn't feel like any of my other hookups. "Uh no, I suppose not."

"Then why should it be an issue for anyone else?" He huffs, his arms crossing over his body.

"I don't think that's how that works. I'm sure lots of people will have something to say about it." Shaking my head in frustration, I take off my mask and drop it with a clang onto the bench, pushing back the hair that falls over my brow.

"Life is too short to live without love, Kris. Besides, if anyone has a problem, send them to me." A wicked gleam winks in his eye and in this one moment I'm unsure if I'm actually afraid of Arthur.

A loud laugh bursts from my chest and Arthur sits, legs dangling, looking mighty pleased with himself.

"Take a break. I'm sure your mom has dinner nearly ready by now. See your boy. This will be here when you return." He gestures to the pieces of metal and electronics that make up the structure of Rudolph's helmet.

The smell of freshly baked pie wafts towards me as I enter the front door. My mother Klaus and Nick all stand chatting animatedly in the kitchen.

I clench my jaw and try to ignore the pang in my heart at watching my mother treat Nick like a son when I have never received the same treatment from Klaus.

"Kris!" My mother beams as she sweeps towards me, embracing me, and I can't help but soften into her warmth. My mother has always been affectionate and that affection has only grown since welcoming Klaus and Nick into our family.

"Hey Mom. I'm just gonna go wash up," I hold my hands out, my blackened fingers are a stark contrast to the white table settings she has out tonight.

I glance over at Klaus and we share a respectful nod, before my eyes fall on Nick, whose mirroring stare is just as brazen as he drinks in my body.

My head quirks to the side, and I let a small smile slip before I shake my head and move to the stairs up to my room. I don't bother turning on the light as I make my way to the adjoining ensuite, leaving the door unlocked and stripping out my grease-covered clothes. I throw them toward the laundry basket, but they land with a thump on the floor next to it.

The copper colored taps are cold in my hand as I turn on the water, adjusting the temperature as hot as it will go. I step under the scalding stream, sighing as the pulsing water relieves some of the tension in my muscles. I scrub my hands and forearms with grit soap, watching the grease wash down the drain, then use my regular pine wash to go over the rest of my body.

After washing my hair, I step out into the steam-filled bathroom and find Nick waiting, his eyes unabashedly scanning my dripping naked body.

I grab a towel but don't bother drying my body. I just ruffle it through my hair, taking my time letting him get his fill.

"Have you found something to your liking, Santa Baby?" I ask. My grin turns devilish as I observe him unconsciously caressing the growing hardness straining against his zipper.

My cock grows under his scrutiny. I drop the towel on the floor next to me and take one long stroke. Running my thumb over the swollen slit I swipe at a bead of moisture, my dick already weeping under his gaze before taking my time, dragging it back up the length.

Nick's eyes don't stray from the movement, his stare almost predatory. I take a step towards the door and flick the lock before stepping back in front of him.

"We seem to have a problem." Nick's eyes quickly flash up to mine in a panic as confusion flicks across his beautiful face.

"Problem?"

"Yes," I growl. "You seem to have far too many clothes on."

Without a second thought, he unbuckles his cream trousers, dropping them and his boxers around his ankles. His thick length jerks under my gaze and I lick my lips in anticipation.

Just as I'm about to collapse to my knees and worship him an idea flashes through my mind. Meeting his gaze, I can't help but grin.

"Do you trust me?" I raise my eyebrows.

"Unequivocally," he whispers, and I lean into him, pressing my lips to his as I wrap my hand firmly around his cock, swallowing his gasp.

He grips the counter as I line up our erections side by side, stroking them in my hand. I bite my lip as the soft skin of his dick rubs against mine.

Fuck, this feels so good.

I can't keep my eyes off of where we touch, noting the differences. Where I am thicker, the olive shade of my skin provides an entrancing contrast to the paleness of his. Despite being slightly longer than me, the most significant contrast is that I am circumcised while he is not.

My arousal bounces with excitement as I line up the tips of our cocks, pressing them together as I run my hand back and forth over the combined length of us both.

I slowly stretch his foreskin with each stroke, taking my time to make sure it is loose enough, before nuzzling the head of my dick inside the tight band of skin.

"Oh fuck," Nick groans at the feeling of my cock rubbing around the shaft of his. As we share a combined sheath, I stroke us together as one.

The more we stroke, the easier it is to slide against him, our cocks simultaneously weep at the friction.

Releasing the counter Nick grabs my face, kissing me. Slow and tender, the same way I run my hand over our enjoined lengths.

Watching the head of my dick move within his foreskin is mesmerizing, and it doesn't take too long until we are both panting and gripping onto each other.

"Do you want me to come inside you, baby?" I groan as my spine tingles, my orgasm quickly building.

He nods, exhaling a quick, "Yes, please." Before grabbing both sides of my face and devouring my mouth.

Together we groan.

His teeth nip at my lip and when my eyes lock onto his, I explode, filling him as my hand stills, keeping us locked together. My cum seeps through my fingers, dripping to the tiled floor as the head of my cock pulses against his.

Gently I squeeze his sack. I caress it and loosen the pressure where we are joined. Pushing him over the edge, and he comes with a muffled whimper as he drops his head to my chest.

We hold each other, panting, my chest swelling with something other than blood, something that feels a lot like ...

A sharp knock at my bedroom door has us stepping away from each other, our now softening cocks dislodging with the movement.

"Kris, dinner is ready." My mom calls from the hallway. "Have you seen Nick?"

"Fuck yeah I have," I whisper and he scowls, before yelling louder for her to hear. "I've been in the shower, Mom."

"Oh right, of course." The sounds of her retreating footsteps have me stepping closer to Nick, wrapping him in a tight embrace which he melts into.

"I guess we need to head to dinner." My lips tilt in a lazy smile as I lean my head to his, kissing his forehead before he leans back against the counter, eyes shining.

"It's never felt like that." And I know he means more than just the mind-blowing sexual experiences. Our relationship keeps strengthening and becoming more. "I'm not ready for this to end, I just can't," Letting out an exacerbated breath, "I don't know. I can't explain it."

His words hit me, and I know exactly how he feels. I don't know when *Operation: Fuck My Big Brother* changed course, but I can't deny that this growing feeling in my chest is becoming harder to ignore.

"Who says this has to end?" I say, surprising even myself. Arthur's words from earlier strengthen my resolve, no one has any say in what we do. We are fucking adults and we can do whatever the fuck we want.

I unlock the bathroom door, step towards my closet and throw on a tee and some sweats, determination fueling my steps. Grabbing his hand, I entwine our fingers as we make my way towards the door.

He pulls me to a stop.

"What are you doing?" Looking down at our joined hands.

"At nearly thirty, I don't think it matters what the fuck Klaus and my mother think of this. I want this. I can't stop thinking about this, us. So what does it matter?"

He winces, and my heart plummets.

He doesn't want this.

Holy shit. I just bared it all to him, and he is taking my heart and shredding it like dead pine needles scattered across the floor in January.

He grips my hand tighter, but I pull mine free from his grasp, running it through my still damp hair.

"Can we just wait until after Christmas, a few more days, let everything die down?" He tries to explain more, but I can't hear him.

He doesn't want anyone to know, he just wants me to be his fuck boy, to experiment. I swing open the door and make a break for the stairs. Nick behind me calls my name, but I don't listen. I need to go.

"Kris?" Klaus' questions from the head of the table.

"I uh, I have to go." I make up some bullshit about an idea of how to fix the fucked up connection, like I have any idea about connections. Klaus almost looks proud at the fact I'm skipping dinner to work.

I can't stop replaying the look on Nick's face as he turned me down. I just throw on my work boots, grab a jacket and stomp out into the snow.

"Kris?" Nick's voice sounds almost broken from the porch.

I turn back to him. "It's all good. I'm glad we got this over with now and not later." I try to disguise the pain in my voice, feigning indifference. But by the drop in his shoulders and the pity in his gaze, he knows.

"Kris, please." He continues to speak, but I can't hear him through the snowstorm that pulses through my ears as I make my way back to the workshop, not stopping till I'm safely locked inside.

Chapter Eight

Nick

Kris didn't end up coming back home last night. The perfectly made bed sits mockingly in his empty room. I had waited in my room till the early hours of the morning, hoping to hear any sound that signaled his return, but I ended up crashing out from sheer exhaustion into a sleep that was anything but restful.

The look on his face when he thought I was turning him down had haunted my dreams.

I needed to explain better, to articulate how my thoughts had transformed into an endless carousel revolving solely around him. That he wasn't alone.

Why didn't I kiss him?

Why hadn't I said anything to reassure him he wasn't alone in his feelings. That I was right there, drowning alongside him.

Instead, I let him walk out and spent the rest of the night silently hating myself over meatloaf and apple pie, listening to my father spout off weather reports and patterns for the big day.

There is just so much on my plate right now, at that moment I couldn't think of adding one more thing to my ever-growing pile.

But Kris isn't just one more thing.

The kitchen is empty when I finally drag myself downstairs. Grateful my father and Carol are already off doing one of the hundred jobs that need to be completed by tomorrow, so I could take a few minutes to sit and wallow in my stupid decisions over a hot cup of coffee.

The looming amount of expectations on me was becoming too much. I need to get through Christmas. Christmas had to be my priority.

I couldn't let millions of children down because I had fallen for a guy. Fuck, not just a guy.

Kris.

My stepbrother.

The guy I have secretly pined over for almost half of my life was finally in my hands and I have already messed it all up.

I groan, my head falling with a thud onto the breakfast bar as the back door opens. I shoot up, turning to the door.

"Kris? ... Carol, hi." Carol gently smiles at me as she enters, arms full of freshly picked mistletoe. I spin back around, trying to hide my disappointment as I sink back onto my stool.

"Nick, are you alright?" Her smile drops as she takes in the wrinkled suit I wore yesterday. After Kris blew out of here like a hurricane, I ate dinner silently before excusing myself and collapsing onto my bed. Not having the heart to do anything else, even though my to do list seems to be ever growing.

Dropping the flowers on the table, she strokes my unshaven face, lips twisting in concern, before taking a mug from the shelf. Pouring herself a cup of coffee, she perches herself on the stool across from me.

Her Christmas sweater jingles as she takes in a mouthful. The knitted version of our festive village sprawled across it, a twinkling backdrop to the large Christmas tree that stands in the foreground. Decorated with small bells where ornaments would normally hang. She waits, hands wrapped around the mug, steam billowing from the cup.

When the silence becomes uncomfortable, my skin begins to itch and I can't stop the words from tumbling out.

"I'm in love with Kris."

Her eyes widen a fraction, but she keeps herself composed as she inhales slowly before standing.

Oh fuck. What did I just do?

She walks out through the kitchen doors and into the dining room and I sigh, leaning my head into my hands as I wait to hear the front door slamming. I imagine the look of devastation on my father's face as Carol tells him how fucked up his son is.

The sound of footsteps draws my head back up and Carol walks towards me, a bottle of my father's top shelf scotch in her hand.

"I feel like this conversation needs something a little stronger than just coffee." A small smile graces her perfectly done up face and a small part of me relaxes at the gesture.

"It's only nine a.m.?" I question, checking my watch. She only shrugs, the response so like Kris my heart twinges.

Bringing my mug to my lips, I drink down the remaining liquid in one mouthful and hold out the mug for her to pour.

She pours a generous amount into my mug before adding the same amount to her steaming coffee, leaving the bottle between us.

"Now, I believe you were in the middle of telling me you had feelings for my son?" Her voice holds no hint of anger or disgust like I had expected, though concern pinches her brow. That is the only sign she shows of discomfort.

"Yes." I take a large mouthful of the amber liquid, warmth running down my throat and filling my stomach as it goes. "I think I've loved him for a while."

"I know." Her voice sounds small, like a delicate whisper floating in the air. My mouth gapes at her response.

"You know?"

"I've known for a long time. The looks, the way your eyes always move to him whenever he enters a room, the hurt that would flash across your face whenever he brought girls home. Yes Nick, I know." She takes a small sip of her coffee while I sit there, dumbstruck.

All this time, I believed I had successfully concealed my feelings for Kris, but evidently my face betrayed me whenever I was in his presence.

"Does my father know?" I ask quietly, wanting to shrivel into my suit.

"Goodness no." She laughs and I release the breath I've been holding. "How does Kris feel?"

Memories of last night come back in a rush, Kris staring into my eyes, our chests heaving as cum dripped on the floor between us. How he rushed to get dressed, determined to come downstairs and tell our parents.

"I want this."

"I can't stop thinking about this, us."

His words echo through my mind as I stare into the same jade eyes across the counter. "I think he loves me, too." I whisper before my shoulders drop and I stare at the marble counter.

"Well, if you think he loves you as well," She mused, the sound of her fingers tapping against the table filling the silence. "Why do you look like your gingerbread house has just collapsed?"

"I messed up." I exhale, still not ready to look into the same jade eyes that I watched slowly break in front of me last night.

Her voice is calm and matter-of-fact. "I'm sure it isn't anything a little icing can't fix."

"I..." Looking up to her face, wincing. "I'm not sure."

"Well, maybe this is a conversation you need to have with Kris. A simple conversation has the power to resolve a surprising amount of problems." She smiles as she downs the last of her coffee. "Now last I saw my son, he was out with Rudolph trying on that fancy new helmet. That might be a good place to start."

She stands patting me on the shoulder and turns to bunch up the flowers pooling across the small table.

"You're not disappointed?" She immediately stops, turning on the balls of her feet to face me as her jade eyes lock onto mine, hardening and now I can see where Kris gets his famous glare from.

"Why would I be upset that such a compassionate and kind hearted man loves my son?" She rests her hands on her hips, looking at me expectantly.

"I, uh I don't know. 'Cause I'm your stepson and isn't this wrong?" Tears well in my eyes and her eyes soften as she reaches for my hand.

"We don't choose who we fall in love with, Nick." She squeezes my hand tightly. "So many people thought I was crazy, packing up our life and moving to literally the top of the world for love, but you know what?" Her eyes gloss with unshed tears as she strokes my face.

"I don't regret a single thing. It brought me here to Klaus. With you. It has been an absolute pleasure getting to watch you grow up into the outstanding man you are today. Tomorrow, when you take off on that sleigh, will be one of the proudest moments of my life."

A single tear tracks down her face, and that is enough to set me off, too. She moves to my side and embraces me tightly.

"Does it feel wrong?" she whispers into my ear.

No, no, it doesn't. Nothing with Kris has ever felt wrong.

My heart has only beaten stronger over the last week, as if it has finally found the place where it belongs. So many emotions flood my system and I can only shake my head into the crook of her neck.

"Well then, I think you have your answer." She kisses the top of my head and packs up her flowers, moving towards the front door.

"What about my father?" I ask, knowing that conversation will not go nearly as well as this one has.

"You leave him to me." She winks before disappearing out the door with a flurry of snow and soft jingles.

Stepping up to the reindeer pen, I take in the expansive snow-covered trees that surround the acreage that the reindeer roam. My family has always insisted on treating the reindeer like royalty. Without them, there would be no Christmas.

Kris stands in the middle of the paddock, dark wash jeans covering his perfectly shaped ass, work boots and black puffy jacket make him stand out in the never ending field of white.

A beanie covers his messy dark locks and his face is buried in the screen of his tablet. He doesn't see my approach.

I lean against the fence and watch as he adjusts settings and looks at the sky, watching Rudolph complete laps, his usual scowl missing from his face. The tawny reindeer's nose is clearly glowing red and bright as he ducks and weaves through clouds. Kris is tracking it all on his monitor, looking in his element.

"It's working." I say, watching in awe.

Looking back at me, he swallows, the scowl returning before taking a few tentative steps closer.

"Yeah." He glances away, looking back at the screen. "I worked through the night and finally got it fitted and ready to go early this morning."

He moves next to me, leaning against the fence post to tilt the screen towards me so I can see the radar data branching out from Rudolph's helmet.

"Seems to run smoothly. I've taken it through three test flights with a single reindeer so far with no glitches."

My hand moves closer to his, brushing gently across the back of his hand, and our little fingers loop together. "I always believed in you."

His finger seems to grip mine tighter and together we both stare out at the field, watching Rudolph land near the other reindeer with a flourish before he struts over to us. He always was the dramatic one of the herd.

"About last night ..." I break our silence.

"Nick, it's fine." He pulls away, the moment broken. Letting go of my finger he moves towards the gate where Rudolph waits for him.

I follow him, my heart screaming I would follow him anywhere he asks. "No it's not. I hurt you and that wasn't my intention."

He looks uncomfortable but doesn't move away as he undoes the helmet before throwing Rudolph a carrot, which he gladly accepts. Turning, he stares at me.

"What was your intention?" Those jade eyes pierce into me. Hard and unyielding.

"I didn't mean to act so poorly. You took me by surprise. For one second, I faced the life I have always dreamed of having and I panicked. Fumbled. You mean so much to me, Kris, and I never meant to make you feel like we could be anything less than everything."

His chest visibly heaves through his coat, his knuckles turn white on the tablet and I worry the screen may break under his vice like grip.

My breath catches as I wait, his eyes searching mine, and I hope he sees nothing but my sincerity.

I want this. I'm all in.

"Everything." He rolls the word over his tongue, testing it out. "You think we can be everything?"

I don't answer him, refusing to look around and double checking who may see us. I step towards him.

Taking his face in my hands, I brush a loose strand of his hair back, his eyes close and he shudders at my touch and I bring his lips to mine. It's gentle, unhurried and filled with all the love that has been growing in me since I was fifteen.

The love of a friend, the love of family, and now into something bigger than us both.

"Okay." His voice is shaky as I rest my forehead on his, and we stand together, holding each other.

"Okay." I reply, knowing this is the beginning of the life I've been waiting for.

"Look at you," Carol croons from the chair in front of my desk, hand pressed to her chest as she tries to hold back tears.

My father stands behind her, placing a hand on her shoulder, giving it a light squeeze as his eyes shine with pride. "It suits you."

Inhaling deeply, I redirect my attention to the elaborate full-length mirror that was brought into my office and placed against the wall. Not recognizing the man that looks back at me.

After spending what little time I could with Kris in the field, I raced back to the barber and had a haircut and beard trim.

With my face framed by a neatly cropped beard, the grays become more prominent in the clipped back style. My hair seamlessly fades to a messy, textured style on the top.

I nearly had the Barber Elf give me my usual shorter haircut, but I enjoyed Kris' firm grip on the longer strands. Easier for him to pull me closer to him. Though a hat made of velvet with a soft white fur trim was currently covering most of it.

I draw my eyes away from the red velvet suit perfectly tailored to fit my body. The Tailor Elves had done a fantastic job of not drawing attention to my stomach, which is a sensitive area for me.

Instead of a thick black belt like my father had, the elves had made me a double-breasted peacoat with big gold buttons sewn in pairs down the center. Lined in the most luxurious fur, it was sure to keep me warm as I traveled through the skies.

Warmth had been a major factor in the design of my outfit. Every piece, meticulously lined to maximize the warmth retention, right down to the white fur cuffing my black glossy boots.

It took my breath away. Although I knew that this moment was coming, my whole life I had spent following my father, learning his role, but still it didn't feel real until this very moment.

In less than twenty-four hours, I would become Santa Claus.

A knock on the door drew my eyes away from the mirror, smiling when familiar jade eyes meet mine.

Kris stands in the doorway, still wearing the clothes he was in out in the field. His beanie is gripped tightly in his hand as he drinks me in, taking his time to savor me.

I can feel the burn of his gaze as it drifts from my eyes slowly down to my boots and back up again, and I silently curse the tailor elves for making this suit so damn warm.

It feels like time has stopped as we stare at each other, completely forgetting that we aren't alone as my body responds to the promise in his eyes, until Carol's knowing cough cuts through my thoughts.

"Doesn't he look handsome, Kris?" Her voice reminds me I haven't told Kris that she knows about us.

Kris expresses his agreement with a grunt, and I reluctantly turn to look at our parents. "We have prepared the sleigh for loading tomorrow morning."

"Excellent." My father's voice booms through my office as he claps his hands together. Releasing Carol's shoulder, he takes a step towards Kris, causing him to tense up in response. However, my father calmly extends his hand in offering. Kris, though guarded, meets my father in the middle, shaking his hand.

"Well done Kris. I know things have been tense between us, more so lately. But I am very proud of all the upgrades and hard work you have put into the sleigh over the last year." Sincerity ringing through his voice, giving Kris' hand one last squeeze before releasing him.

Seeming unsure, Kris shuffles on his feet before muttering a quick thanks. My father nods and turns back to the plans on my desk.

A quick glance at Carol, her wink, hardly subtle as she, too, turns and continues a conversation with my father.

I hadn't noticed Kris moving closer to me, till his low voice sends goosebumps skittering across my body. "I get the suit thing now."

"What?" I ask, meeting his intense gaze as his eyes slowly scan my body, his tongue quickly darts out to moisten his bottom lip.

"I get how Klaus landed my mom in one night." His words are playful, but the smoldering glare in his eyes hints at his true intentions.

The fire in my core comes roaring back to life, and I want nothing more than to kick my parents out of my office and have Kris take me over my desk. Paperwork flying everywhere as he grinds into me, claiming me as his own.

I cough, adjusting myself as he smirks, knowing he has me hot and bothered. Brushing past me, our little fingers linking for a second before he continues forward to our parents.

"I'm gonna go clean up the workshop. After this week, it looks like a bomb went off in there," he says, leaning in to give Carol a quick kiss on the cheek.

"Okay sweetie. Will you be joining us for dinner?" Her voice full of hope as she glances back and forth between her son and my father. I know her hope is for them to put this tension behind them.

A tight-lipped nod is his answer, and she gives him a beaming smile, patting his cheek.

Turning back to me, I swallow as he moves closer, speaking in a hushed tone so only I can hear.

"Workshop. Tonight. Bring the suit, hat and all." My eyes widen as his smirk turns devilish.

My balls tighten as my pants, perfectly tailored, feel too tight. Knuckles grazing over me, he quickly glances back at our parents. My eyes flick up too, noting how they still discuss the loading plans for the morning.

His hot breath skates over my skin as his tongue draws a hot, wet line up my neck.

I shiver at his words, like a phantom hand, curl around my already straining length.

"Tomorrow you might be Santa, but tonight you'll be sitting on my lap."

Chapter Nine

Nick

December 24th

THE WORLD MOVES AT a rapid pace around me. Elves stand in production lines, loading cargo, ensuring everything is ready for my take off in the next three hours.

My mind, though, stays trapped in Kris' workshop. Flashes of last night pull my attention away from the bustling crowd.

Sitting on Kris' lap in the sleigh's cockpit, back pressed to his chest as his cock slammed up into me. His grunts of "Fuck me Santa" playing on repeat alongside the sound of our mingled groans.

If I look closely, I'm sure I could see marks where my fingers have indented into the dashboard as he pumped his seed deep into me, the feeling causing my own to shoot all over the controls.

It took us until the early hours of this morning to drag our hands away from each other, then another hour to clean up all the mess we made in the freshly polished sleigh. My father would be mortified if the sleigh came out drenched in our mingled cum for takeoff tomorrow.

Should I have stayed up fucking Kris most of the night? Probably not.

Even with only five hours of sleep and the long journey ahead, I couldn't bring myself to regret spending another night with him, worshiping each other's bodies.

My eyes find him across the runway, strapping in the reindeer. Even from here I can see his hair still disheveled, evidence of the hours I spent running my hands through it.

He pauses at each animal, ensuring their new helmets are secure before leaning in to whisper into each of their ears.

When he finishes, his face lifts and he searches the crowd before his gaze falls on me. A small smile crosses his lips before he turns back to Arthur and together they run through the final safety checks on the sleigh.

Even after he has returned to his work, my body remains attuned to his presence, humming with awareness.

I stand amidst the gentle snowfall, my heart clenching as I watch the flurry of activity surrounding me.

This is real.

Inhaling deeply, I take one last look at Kris before jumping into action. I have a few last checks I need to oversee before I need to get back into my suit and make my way up to the village center for the annual farewell town breakfast.

"It suits you." Carol's voice startles me from my thoughts, her words echo my father's. I stand at my office window looking out at the now empty workshop. After months of this workshop overflowing with toys and elves, hard at work, the now baron space feels strange.

I run my hands down my suit for the twentieth time since I put it on. I force a tight-lipped smile, my face unable to hide the nerves coursing through me, but she wraps me in the type of hug that only she can give. Instantly a wave of comfort washes over me.

"You'll be back in no time. It will be over before you know it and you'll be wondering how it went by so fast." She offers and I nod, not knowing what to say.

I have stood here for the last hour questioning my ability to get this job done. If I could be as good of a Santa as every other that has come before me. Could I live up to the legacy set by my forefathers?

She loosens her grip on me, but her hands linger on my face, caressing it gently, her touch warm and comforting, as tears well up in her eyes. "I am so proud of you."

"What if I mess up?" I whisper, my voice barely audible, scared that someone might hear me. I look away, not ready to handle the look of disappointment on her face.

"Nicolas." She scolds me as her grip on my face grows tighter. "Do you really think your father never worried about making a mistake?"

When my eyes come back to her, she stares at me, head cocked to the side and a slight smile tips up her mouth. I shrug, burying my hands in my pockets.

"Every morning for the last fifteen years, your father has put on his suit, looked in the mirror and asked me the same question."

"What did you tell him?" Her smile grows as she grasps one of my hands, dragging me over to the ornate mirror that still stands against the wall in my office, and pushing me in front of it.

"I told him that to the world he may be Santa Claus, but to me he was just Klaus. That no matter what happens out there, here, we still love you."

I stare at myself. The red suit, with its vibrant color, shines brightly under the bright office fluorescents. Out of the corner of my eye, I can see my hat sitting limply on my desk.

Carol notices where I am staring and moves to pick it up. Walking it over to me, I inhale deeply as she lifts onto her toes to place it securely on my head.

"From today you are Santa Claus, but to us you will always be our Nick. No matter what happens, out there, here, we will always love you." A tear falls down my cheek at her words and I turn, enveloping her in a hug, pressing my forehead into her shoulder.

"Thank you."

"Come now, my boy, everyone is desperately awaiting breakfast and you know how your father likes to kick this morning off with a speech that goes until the new year." A snort escapes me as she pats me on the back. His speeches do usually drag on for an unreasonable amount of time.

As we make our way out, I pray he is already near the end of his speech, although the thought of standing up to address everyone has my stomach churning and my palms sweating.

"Ah, there he is, the man of the hour." My father's voice booms across the square.

My father has always made the residents of the village feel like an extended part of our family. Everyone is welcome at our table and this morning feels more like a big family reunion than a work breakfast.

For everyone here today, their work is done. After months of planning, prepping, and executing, the workers have completed their work by making the presents, carefully wrapping them, and storing them in the sleigh ready for delivery.

With meticulous planning, the team has ensured that no child is missing from their carefully designed routes, and the reindeer have been diligently honing their skills during training sessions.

Kris and Arthur have spent months crafting the upgrades needed to ensure my trip goes smoothly.

From here on out, it's up to me.

The crowd bursts into a symphony of cheers, with hands stretching out towards me, shaking my hand and giving me encouraging pats on the back as I move towards the front.

Their enthusiasm fills me, and I straighten, a smile spreading across my face as I greet them back.

When I reach the front, Kris stands waiting alongside the stage, his jade eyes filled with something I only hope is real, making my stomach flutter with much more than nerves. He gives me a quick wink and nods towards the stage, urging me to go on.

Carol joins him, and he wraps his arm around her shoulder as she leans into him. My father meets me at the top of the stairs, shaking my hand, giving me a warm hug and I take a second to revel in this moment, soaking it in.

Festive ornaments beautifully decorate the stage, and at its center stands a single microphone adorned with a mistletoe garland, patiently waiting for me.

"Friends, family. Welcome. I know my father has probably already thanked you for your hard work this year, but I wanted to thank you all as well." Eager eyes look back up at me, families grouped together, hugging and holding each other.

"Although children around the world will go to sleep tonight, eagerly awaiting my arrival. I want to acknowledge that there is no me without all of you. Although I may be the representative of our work, it is the tireless efforts of each and every one of you that give Christmas its true meaning."

Claps ring out across the crowd. With a slight nod of his head, my father encourages me to go on.

"From the bottom of my heart, I thank you. This year has been a year of change for us and though the path ahead may not always be easy, it will be one we can all travel ..." My eyes drift to the side of the stage, where Kris waits, his intense gaze locked on me, "together."

He gives me a barely perceptible nod, which gives me the strength to turn back to the waiting crowd. "Now I won't keep you from Mabel's breakfast feast. Goodness knows you have earned it. Please, celebrate with me and my family and then join us for takeoff." I motion towards my family as my father and Carol make their way towards the crowd. Kris choosing to linger behind, waiting for me.

As the crowd disperses, moving towards the endless trays of every breakfast item one could think of. I stuff a hand into the pocket of my suit as I move towards him, pulled by an invisible thread, linking us together.

"Impressive speech, Santa." His finger subtly trails along mine as we walk side by side towards the tables.

We take our time as everyone around us fills their plates with bacon, eggs and pancakes. They pass around mugs of what I assume is spiked hot cocoa, and I politely decline when one is handed out for me.

"Impressive?"

"Well, not as impressive as your ass in that suit, but I think you made an impact." He shrugs, giving me a sly grin as his fingers move to interlace with mine but he withdraws his hand, stepping ever so slightly away, when a worker and their family stop me. I frown at the loss of contact but slip back into a tight smile as they thank me for my effort this year and wish me a safe trip with a tight handshake.

When the family wanders back into the throng of people, Kris steps closer and his warmth solidifies my resolve. I don't want to hide us. This will be difficult for some to understand, but I hope, with time, it is something people can grow to accept.

Or they won't. I don't know what I would do in that case, but my heart thumps to a beat that doesn't match anyone but Kris.

I have a feeling that most people in the village would warmly embrace and accept Kris and me.

When it comes to sharing the news, there is only one person who I worry about the most.

My father.

The runway lights are lit with red and green as my father moves the sleigh into position. The excited crowd eagerly gathers along the pathway to bid me farewell.

From the sidelines, this moment has always felt like putting the star on top of the tree, stepping back to enjoy the beauty, reveling in a sense of accomplishment after all of the hard work as we waited for my father to wish us a Merry Christmas from the skies.

Now I stood on the other side, a different level of hard work in my future. My father lingers next to the cockpit, his hand on the shell of the sleigh, lost in his own memories.

"I know I haven't always been there for you. This role is incredibly demanding, as I'm sure you will learn. Though I couldn't be prouder of the man you have become." Tears well in his eyes as he strokes the sleigh, a vulnerable smile tipping up his lips as he glances down the runway at the row of reindeer, weighting for my go.

"Losing your mother was one of the hardest moments in my life and I know for many years I threw myself into this cockpit, hoping one day that I could find some magical spark for us. Something to bring us back together."

He stops glancing over to Kris and Carol huddled next to each other; I smile as Kris tries to wrap Carol in his jacket and the two playfully bicker with matching smiles.

Though I still worry I am not good enough for this role. Carol's words ring in my mind as Kris looks up and smiles wide straight at me.

Here I will always be just Nick, and I am loved.

"They are two very special people." His words pull me back and I nod.

"They are."

My father sighs as he scrubs his hand along his face, looking like he has something he wants to say. I wait for his words but they don't come, just a frustrated sigh as he looks back at our two favorite people.

As he hands me the reins, I can feel the weight of the role he has cherished for the last five decades.

He lets out a shaky breath as he pats me on the shoulder and makes his way to stand with Carol and Kris.

With one last glance at the row of people lining the path, I feel a sense of unity and support from my entire community.

Moving up the stairs, I settle into the cockpit, adjusting all the belts and clicking the safety features to active.

I close my eyes and let the crisp December wind brush against my face as I exhale slowly.

I am ready for this.

I can do this.

My eyes snap open, there was just one thing I need to do first.

With a click of the belt, I was out of the cockpit, running towards the one person I needed in this moment.

"Nick, what are you doing?" Teddy shrieks as I run past him. "In ninety seconds, you will be officially behind schedule."

"This won't take long." I yell back, slowing to a jog as I near the path. Mummers from the crowd whisper back and forth, but I ignore them all. I need Kris to know I am in this just as much as he is.

A knowing smirk flits across his face as I draw closer, but the bob of his Adam's apple and the quick glance he gives the waiting crowd hints at his nervousness.

"I couldn't leave without a proper goodbye." I rasp, almost out of breath from the short run across the field and my nearness to him. His scent invades my senses and I breathe him in deep.

"And what is a proper goodbye?" His eyes dart between my eyes before dropping to my lips.

This time it was my turn to smirk. Grabbing his jacket, I pull him to me as I crush our lips together. The crowd surrounding us gasps at our embrace. My father's shocked gasp, louder than them all.

I push them all out, not wanting to ruin this moment with Kris. Carol's whispered hushes and we will talk about this later float across the air, but Kris presses himself against me and we melt into each other's warmth.

Pulling back, I'm now breathless for a different reason. Kris' gaze softened as he drank me in.

"Everything starts now." I whisper, and he smiles as he presses another gentle kiss against my lips.

"I'll see you when you get home." His words are soft as his arms encase me.

"So you aren't done with me?" My eyebrow quirks in question and his smile deepens into his signature smirk.

"Oh no, Santa Baby. I am no way near done with you." Placing one last searing kiss on my lips, before he turns me toward the sleigh. He chuckles against my ear. "Go before Theodore has a coronary that you aren't already flying over the South Pacific."

Looking back over to the Head Elf, his face is now almost as red as my suit, a sharp Christmas contrast against his green and gold outfit.

"I'd like you back in one piece and right now, Teddy looks about ready to commit homicide." His chuckle deepens as his hot breath crests against my ear. The middle-aged elf stamping impatiently next to the sleigh, but I can't help but smile.

"I'll be home for Christmas." I say to him over my shoulder as I make my way back to the sleigh, casting a quick glance over towards our parents, Carol's hand clenching my father's arm. She gives me a wink and a nod before patting him soothingly on the arm and whispering in his ear.

"I'll be waiting." Kris' words float over to me on a frosted breeze and I smile as I buckle myself back in.

With a powerful exhale, I bellow out my command; the sound echoing through the air. "Now, Dasher! Now, Dancer! Now, Prancer and Vixen! On Comet! On, Cupid! On, Donner and Blitzen."

With a jolt, the reindeer stamp their hooves. Rudolph's nose glows brighter as he tugs and spurs the group forward.

The blustery wind whips across my face, and I let out a laugh as I feel the Christmas magic pour through me. A few strides later at the sound of my whistle, the reindeer leap into the air, pulling the sleigh and me with them.

Pulling the reins tight around my gloved hands, I direct the reindeer around in a circle. The group waiting below look like tiny ants from this height. I bring us back over the runway, just like my father used to.

I bellow into the cold winter air one more time before the reindeer whisk me away on our journey.

"Happy Christmas to all, and to all a good night."

Acknowledgements

Where to begin.

This journey has been a wild ride of insanity and one I had not expected to take. For so many years I have obsessed over romance and fantasy novels, spending way too many nights bleary eyed, but refusing to put it down and actually go to sleep.

Never in a million years would I have guessed that the writing bug would not only bite me but latch on and refuse to let go.

Though my name (well not really) may be on the cover of this book there is no way I could have gotten this far without a whole village full of people cheering me on.

These people have believed in me through all of my self-doubt, been my shoulder to cry on when things weren't making sense or given me inspiration on a day-to-day basis with their messages and unending supply of TikTok videos.

Your laughter and love has given me a safe space to share my thoughts and fears and you champion me every day, even when I don't feel worthy.

To my husband, my muse (as he likes to call himself), you have loved me for almost half of my life and without you, I wouldn't be me. You have been my number one fan on every single ADHD adventure I have gone on from crochet to weightlifting. I'm sure you were glad when I picked up a static hobby like reading, though now I'm sure you and our bank account are both shaking your heads. Every day you give me the strength to keep pushing and striving towards my goals. I hope one day you can be my trophy husband when I make it big.

To my daughters, though I will be dead before you are ever allowed to read my romance novels. Thank you for bringing so much joy to our lives, life is never dull with you both around and I could never imagine my life without your smiles, jokes and the never-ending twerking that occurs on a daily basis. I have been so lucky to have been given two amazingly smart and determined daughters and I cannot wait to witness the lives you will both carve out for yourselves. Follow your dreams, my babies.

My besties. Jamie, Jill, Jess and Amy. I would not know what I would do if I didn't have you all in my life. Though some of you I have known for a lifetime and the others only the last few years. You are a family, like no other. Thank you for listening to me drone on about ideas, cover concepts and plot twists. For reading every page of anything I've sent you, even when it didn't make sense. For your feedback and unwavering support and helping me believe I'm not crazy to strive for this dream. I love you all.

To my editor Ash from AVA Book Editing. Your support and guidance over the last seven months has been indescribable. Your cheers of support and much needed advice has helped this baby author navigate not only the editing process but also the entire self-publishing world. Thank you for the amazing work that you do, turning my jumbled mess of words into such a beautiful love story.

To Georgia of Pixel and Quill Studio, my beautiful cover designer. Thank you for spending so much time developing such an amazing cover. What you have created has turned out better than I could have ever dreamed up myself and I couldn't have done it without your kindness and understanding.

Lastly, I would like to thank Chloe. *Supreme Leader*. A few years ago, you created a Facebook book club that changed my life. This group allowed me to meet some of the absolute best women and create lifelong friendships with people that I would have otherwise never met, in turn becoming a huge catalyst for this dream of mine.

Thank you to everyone who is reading my novel. I am so honoured that you have spent your precious time reading this little love story. I hope you have loved it as much as I do.

M.K x

About the author

M.K Vindictiv is a Diet Coke addicted, smut-loving author who lives in Adelaide, Australia.

When her nose isn't buried in a book, she can be found spending quality time with her husband and two daughters or enthusiastically supporting her beloved Bruins.

In an effort to escape the pressures of adult life, she rediscovered her love of reading. After spending years immersing herself in emotionally traumatising romance novels, she found herself completely captivated by the intense emotional rollercoaster these stories offered their readers.

Stumbling onto her own idea, she fumbled her way through the often-difficult journey of becoming a novelist and fell in love with storytelling.

Through her writing, she channels her love of reading into creating romance novels that have the power to make readers experience a blend of both pain and love. She hopes one day readers will be just as enthralled in her stories as she is.

To keep up to date with future releases and what's going on in the Vindictiv world, please scan the QR code below

@MKVINDICTIV.AUTHOR